INORGANIC CHEMISTRY

Dr. Rajaram Dhok

Savitribai Phule Pune University Affiliated
Agricultural Development Trust's
Shardabai Pawar Mahila College, Baramati, Pune,
India

Publisher:

Dr. Rajaram Dhok

Shardanagar, Malegaon Bk.

Tal – Baramati, Dist- Pune

Maharashtra, India

PIN - 413115

Website: www.rajaramdhok.com

E mail:- dhokrp@gmail.com

Contact: +91 9921214790

Copyright © 2021 With Publisher

All rights reserved

First Edition: **February 2021**

ISBN:

Printers Details: Amazon Digital Services LLC-KDP Print US.

Type Setting and Cover Page Designer:
Mr. Vaibhav Dhok

Vaibhav Editing Studio

E mail:- vrdhok@gmail.com

Contact: +91 8485887700

DEDICATION

This book is dedicated to the memory of my
beloved wife Alka

CONTENTS

CHAPTER 7: MOLECULAR ORBITAL THEORY OF COORDINATION COMPLEXES 81

CHAPTER 8: MOLECULAR ORBITAL THEORY OF COVALENT

ACKNOWLEDGMENTS

I consider it as a great privilege to express my deep sense of gratitude to **Mr. Rajendra Power**, Chairman, Agricultural   Development Trust, Baramati and **Mrs. Sunanda Pawar**, Trustee, Agricultural Development Trust, Baramati for constant encouragement and motivations for writing the book. I offer my sincere thanks to **Prof. Nilesh Nalawade,** CEO, Agricultural Development Trust for his continuous guidance and encouragement.

I am thankful to **Dr. S. J. Sathe**, Principal, Shardabai Pawar Mahila College, Shardanagar, Baramati, Pune for co-operation in academic work.   I   also express my sincere gratitude to **Dr. S. V. Mahamuni**, Vice Principal, Shardabai Pawar Mahila College, Shardanagar, Baramati, Pune for co-operation and constant encouragement for writing the book. I offer my sincere thanks to **Prof. R. B. Deshmukh, Prof. A. S. Kadam, Dr. paramita Jadhav**. I offer my sincere thanks to **Dr. P. E. More,** Head, Dept. of Chemistry **and all other staff of chemistry,** Shardabai Pawar Mahila College, Shardanagar, Baramati for continuous support and help during the work.

Sacrifice of my son **Vaibhav** and daughter-in-law **Pooja;** brother **Raghunath Dhok** during the tenure of the work is highly appreciable. I acknowledge to my all friends and well-wishers whom i may not have mentioned here but have been always helpful at appropriate time. I Dedicate this book to my beloved wife Alka, her constant encouragement and motivations are constantly with me.

Dr. Rajaram Dhok

FOREWORD

Inorganic Chemistry book covers the basic approach of various coordination chemistry theories and molecular orbital theory of covalent bonding. This book fulfills the need of graduate and post graduate students of chemistry. Book is written in eight chapters. The all contents of book are included in the syllabus of TYBSc Chemistry of Savitribai Phule Pune University, India.

First chapter written on the introduction of coordination chemistry. It covers the historical development in coordination chemistry. Various terms used in coordination chemistry is defined here. Nomenclature of coordination complexes with suitable examples is explained in this chapter. Formation constant, types of formation constant, factors affecting the stability of complexes and various applications of coordination complexes in analytical field, industrial field and biological uses are given in brief.

Werner's theory is prescribed in second chapter. Postulates of Werner's theory, is given here. The comparison of ions in two coordination spheres with suitable examples is explained here. How charges of complex ion are calculated is described in this chapter.

Coordination complexes shows different isomers. In the third chapter, types isomerism in coordination complexes is given in detail with suitable examples. In structural isomerism, various types such as Ionization isomerism, Hydrate isomerism, Ligand isomerism, Linkage isomerism, Coordination position isomerism is prescribed. Stereoisomerism or space isomerism shows geometrical or cis-trans isomerism is given with suitable diagrams. Geometrical isomerism in square planar complexes and octahedral complexes are explained in this chapter. Optical or mirror image isomerism in square planar complexes, tetrahedral complexes and octahedral complexes were given with suitable diagrams.

Chapter four cover with Sidgwick theory. This theory is explained with various examples of Sidgwick model. Definition of EAN and limitations of Sidgwick model is also given in the chapter.

Valence Bond Theory (VBT) for coordination complexes is given in fifth chapter. This theory covers, assumptions of VBT, Concept of hybridization, bonding in tetrahedral, square planar, octahedral complexes is explained according to Pauling theory with the help of suitable examples. Inner and outer orbital complexes, Electroneutrality principle, multiple bonding and limitations of VBT is prescribed in this chapter.

Chapter six is covered with Crystal Field Theory (CFT) of coordination complexes. This chapter includes, assumptions of CFT, shapes of d orbitals, group theoretical symbols for various orbitals. Splitting of d orbitals, application of CFT to octahedral complexes is explained here. Strong and weak ligand field splitting concept is given with distribution of electrons in d orbitals. Crystal field stabilization energy (CFSE) is calculated for d^1 to d^{10} case. Various evidences for the formation of CFSE is explained with suitable example. Crystal field spectra and measurement of 10 Dq is given with example, various factors affecting magnitude of 10 Dq is given with suitable examples. How magnetic property is measured with the help of CFT is described here. Jahn-Teller distortion is very important in CFT, it is given in this chapter. Application of CFT to square planar complexes, tetrahedral complexes, octahedral complexes is explained in detail with various d cases. Spectrochemical and Nephelauxetic effect is described with its series. Limitations of CFT is also noted at the end of chapter.

Chapter seven covers the Molecular Orbital Theory (MOT) of coordination complexes. In this chapter postulates of MOT are given at the start, then MO treatment of bonding is explained with MO energy level diagram. MO energy level diagrams for various coordination complexes is drawn. Effect of π bonding on stability of coordination complexes is explained with suitable diagram. Ligand field theory and charge transfer spectra is briefly described at the end of chapter.

Chapter eight covers the molecular orbital theory of covalent bonding. In this chapter introduction about valence bond theory of covalent bonding is given in brief. Comparison of VBT and MOT is noted here. Linear combination of atomic orbital (LCAO) concept for covalent bonding is explained in this chapter. How bonding and antibonding molecular orbitals formed is explained with suitable example. Formation of molecular orbital diagram is given with diagram. Combinations of s-s, s-p, p-p, p-d orbitals are explained with suitable diagrams. Molecular orbital energy level diagram for H_2^+, H_2, He_2^+, He_2, Li_2, Be_2, B_2, C_2, N_2, O_2, F_2, CO, NO, HCl, CO_2, NO_2 were explained with suitable diagram in six steps.

This book is mainly useful for the students of Savitribai Phule Pune University, India students, the all the contents are included in the syllabus of TYBSc Chemistry.

February 2021   **Dr. Rajaram Dhok**

CHAPTER 1: INTRODUCTION TO COORDINATION CHEMISTRY

1.1 Introduction

Coordination compounds are special class of compounds in which co-ordinate bond is present. These compounds contain a central atom or ion usually a metal. it is surrounded by a species i.e. ions or molecules. Metal complex may be a cation or an anion or non- ionic or neutral molecules. The total charge depends on the sum of the charges of central atom and the surrounding ions and molecules. Coordination complexes requires the following conditions for their formation.

i)   The metal ion or atom should containsufficient number of empty orbitals for bond formation and

ii) Atom, ions or molecules should contain a lone pair of electrons which they can donate to the metal atom or ion.

Scientist had prepared large number of inorganic compounds, some of them compounds are called double salts, hydrates etc. they are also called as molecular or addition compound. some of these compounds showed a tendency to retain their identity in solid state and lose the same in solution state.

Compounds like $KCl.MgCl_2.6H_2O$ (carnallite), $FeSO_4.(NH_4)_2SO_4.H_2O$ (ferrous ammonium sulphate), $K_2SO_4.(Al_2SO_4)_3.24H_2O$ (potassium alum) etc. are called double salts. In the aqueous solution they try to retain their identity and give the test for constituent ions.

However compounds like $K_4[Fe(CN)_6]$ (potassium ferrocyanide), $K_3[Fe(CN)_6]$ (potassium ferricyanide) are called coordination complex, because in their aqueous solution they lose their identity and do not show the test for individual ions like Fe^{2+}, Fe^{3+} and CN^- ions. But gives test for k^+ and $[Fe(CN)_6]^{3-}$ and $[Fe(CN)_6]^{4-}$. Table 1.1 shows the difference between double salt and complex salt.

Table 1.1: Difference between double salt and complex salt

Double Salt	Complex Salt
1) Exist only in crystalline state	1) Exist both in crystalline and solution state
2) All constituent ions can be detected	2) All constituent ions can't be detected
3) Individual compounds do not lose their identity in solution	3) Individual compounds lose their identity in solution
4) Absence of complex ion	4) Presence of complex ion
5) Examples - Carnalite $KCl.MgCl_2.6H_2O$ Potash alum $K_2SO_4.(Al_2SO_4)_3.24H_2O$	5) Examples – potassium ferrocyanide $K_4[Fe(CN)_6]$ potassium ferricyanide $K_3[Fe(CN)_6]$

1.2 Historical development of coordination chemistry

Historical development of progress in coordination chemistry is observed in three stages.

 i) The latter part of 18th century to 1893,

 ii) The Werner's era 1893 to 21940 and

 iii) The modern era 1940 onwards

It impossible to state exactly, when the first coordination compound was discovered. One of the earliest recorded compound is Prussian blue - an artist colour, $KCN.Fe(CN)_2.Fe(CN)_3$. It was obtained accidentally in 1704 by a colour marker Diesbach in Berlin. He heated animal waste and sodium carbonate in an iron vessel and got a blue-coloured compound. This complex compound can be prepared today by mixing ferric salt with potassium hexacyanoferrate.

In 1753, Macquer prepared potassium hexacyanoferrate by reacting Prussian blue with alkali. In 1798, Tassaert prepared Orange coloured complex compound hexaamminecobalt(III) chloride. $CoCl_3.6NH_3$ was obtained by mixing solution of cobalt chloride with aqueous ammonia. Between 1800 to 1850 large number of complex compound where prepared. Some of them were $K_3[Fe(CN)_6]$ (in 1822), $[Pt(NH_3)_4] [Pt(Cl_4]$ (in 1828), $Na_2[Fe(CN)_5NO]$ (in 1849).

1.3 Definition of Various Terms

(1) Coordination compounds: A coordination compound is complex compound in which the **number of bonds formed by the central atom or ion is greater than that expected from the usual valency considerations**. The extra groups or ions are attached to the metal by coordination bonds which the attached group (L) is the donor. For e.g. potassium ferrocyanide, $k_3 [Fe (CN)_6]$. The usual valency of Fe is three but it forms six bonds with CN- ions. Coordination compounds may be either cationic or anionic or both or neutral. For e.g.

    (a)   Complex cation- $[Cu(NH_3)_4]^{+2}$
    (b)   Complex anion- $[Fe(CN)_6]^{-3}$
    (c)   Complex cation and anion - $[Co(NH_3)_6]^{+3} [Cr(CN)_6]^{-3}$
    (d)   Neutral - $[Co(NH_3)_3Cl_3]$

(2) Complex ion: A complex ion is **charged species formed when a metal atom or ion is directly attached to a group of neutral molecules and/ or ions called ligands**. The complex ion is indicated by enclosing the formula for the ion in a square bracket. Example are,

(i) $[Cu(NH_3)_4]^{+2}$ neutral ammonia molecule are attached to Cu^{+2} ion.

(ii) $[Co(NO_2)_6]^{-3}$ negative NO_2^{-2} ions are attached to Co^{+3} ion and

(iii) $[Co(NH_3)_3Cl_3]$ both negative ion Cl- as well as neutral NH3 molecules are attached to Co^{+3} ion.

(3) Central atom: It is the **metal atom generally present in neutral coordination compounds to which two or more neutral molecules are**

attached, e.g. $Ni(CO)_4$, $Fe(CO)_5$ --- etc.

(4) Central ion: It is the **metal ion in the complex to which two or more neutral molecules or anions are attached**. e.g. in the complex ion $[Co(NH_3)_5Cl]^{2+}$, the cobalt ion is the central ion to which NH_3 molecules and Cl- ion are attached.

(5) Ligand: Any **atom, ion or molecule which is capable of donating a pair of electrons to the central metal atom or ion is called a ligand or a coordinating group**. Ligand contain a electron pair known as donor atom or donor site. Common monodentate ligands are shown in table 1. They are classified according to the number of donor atoms present in it. If ligand contain only one donor atom, it is called monodentate or unidentate ligand. If two or more donor atoms are present in the molecule, it is called polydentate ligand. Polydentate ligands are shown in table 2.

(6) Coordinate or dative bond: Coordinate bond is a **special type of covalent bond in which two shared electrons are contributed by only one of the two atoms linked together**. The atom contributing the electron pair is known as a donor while the atom which accepts this electron pair is known as acceptor. The coordinate bond is usually shown by a short arrow ($\rightarrow$). The arrow head is directed from the donor atom to the acceptor atom.

(7) Coordination number (C.N.): The number of **ligands, which are directly attached to the central metal atom or ion,** is known as coordination number of the complex.

Table 1: Common Monodentate Ligands

Common Name	IUPAC Name	Formula
Fluoro	Fluoro	F^-
Chloro	Chloro	Cl^-
Bromo	Bromo	Br^-
Iodo	iodo	I^-
Azido	azido	N_3^-
Cyano	cyano	CN^-
Thiocyano	thiocyanato or thiocyanato-S	SCN^-
Isothiocano	isothiocyanato or thiocyanato-N	NCS^-
Hydroxo	hydroxo	OH^-
Aqua	aquo	H_2O
Carbonyl	carbonyl	CO
Thiocarbonyl	thiocarbonyl	CS
Nitrosyl	nitrosyl	NO^+
Nitro	Nitro (N bonded)	NO_3-
Nitrito	nitrito (O bonded)	ONO^-
Pyridine	pyridine	py
Ammine	ammine	NH_3
Methyl amine	methylamine	CH_3NH_2
Methylcyanide	methylcyanide	CH_3CN
Methylisocyanide	methylisocyanide	CH_3NC
Amido	amido	NH_2-

Table 2: Common polydentate Ligands

Dentate Type	IUPAC Name	Abbreviation	Formula
Bidentate	ethylenediamine	en	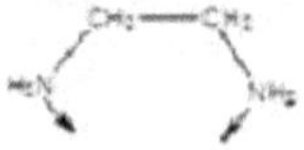
	2-2' dipyridyl	dipy	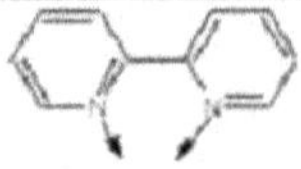
	glycinato	gly	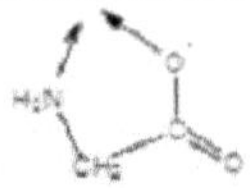
	acetylacetonato	acac	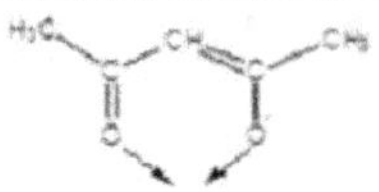
	dimethylglyoximato	DMG	
	oxalate	ox	
Tridentate	diethylenetriamine	dien	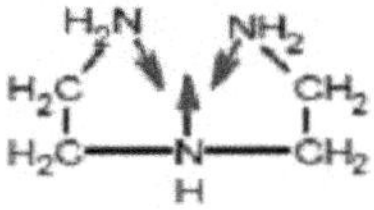
Tetradentate	Triethylene tetramine	trien	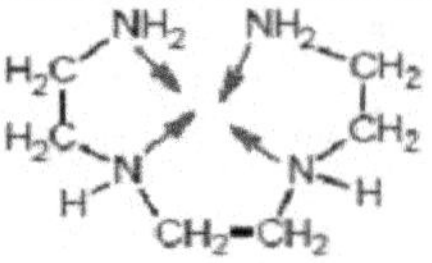
Pentadentate	Ethylenediamine triacetato	EDTA	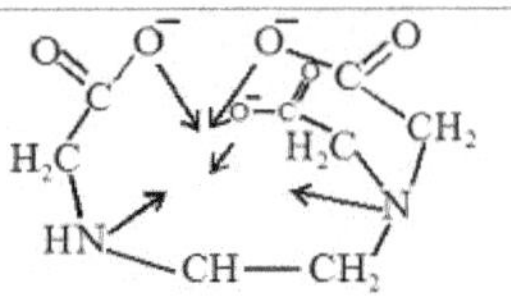
Hexadentate	Ethylenediamine tetracetato	EDTA	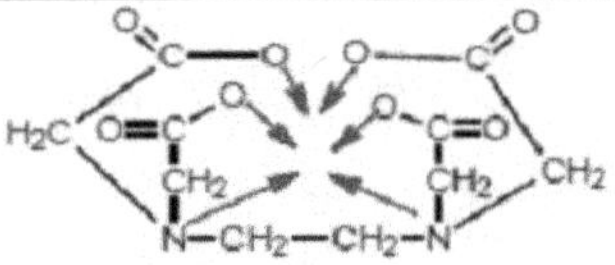

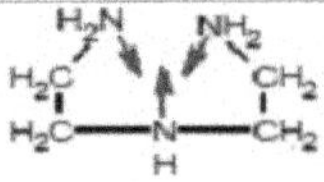

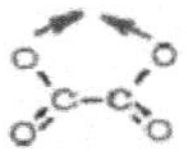

1.4 Nomenclature of Coordination Compounds

Rules for nomenclature:

1) Anionic complex ions: If the complex ion is anonic i.e. containing cation and a complex anion, then the cation is named first followed by the full name of the anion. The names of cation and anion are separated by a space. e.g.

$$K_2[PtCl_6] \text{ - potassium hexachloroplatinate (IV)}$$
$$K_3[Fe(CN)_6] \text{ - potassium hexacyanoferrate (III)}$$

In first example, in the square bracket, there is an anion Cl-. There are six such Cl- ions. so, it is named first as hexachloro. The metal Pt is not free. It is in the square bracket. Hence it is not named simply as platinum but it is named as platinate, since square bracket carries a negative charge i.e. name of the metal ends in –ate.

2) Cationic complex ions: If the complex is cationic i.e. containing a cationic complex ion and anion, then the names of the ligands present in the square bracket are written according to the order given in rule 4. Then the names of the metal are written with its valency in a small bracket. The names of anion, outside the square bracket are then written. e.g.

$$[Co(NH_3)_6]Cl_3 \text{ - hexaamminecobalt(III) chloride.}$$

$[Cr(H_2O)_4Cl_2]Cl$ - dichlorotetraaquochromium(III) chloride. For some metals, their lattin names are used e.g. copper (cuprum) - cuprate, iron (ferrum) - ferrate, lead (plumbum) - plumbate, gold (aurum)- aurate, silver (argentums) - argentate.

3) Non-ionic complexes: Non-ionic or molecular complexes are given a one word name. The name of the negative ligand is written first, then the name of the neutral is written. The name of the metal is written at the end. The valency of the metal is shown in a small bracket in a roman figure. Examples-

$$[Co(NH_3)_3Cl_3] \text{ - trichlorotriamminecobalt (III)}$$
$$[Pt(NH_3)_2Cl_4] \text{ - tetrachlorodiammineplatinum (IV)}$$

4) Order of listing ligands: If there are two or more type of ligands present in the complex in the square bracket, then the order of naming is-
(i) negative ligands,
(ii) neutral ligands and

(iii) positive ligands.

After naming ligands in the square bracket, the name of the metal in the square bracket is written with its valency in a small bracket. Then the name of the negative ion outside the square bracket is written. e.g.

$[Co(NH_3)_4(NO_2)(Cl)]\ ClO_4$ - chloronitrotetraamminecobalt(III) perchlorate.

If there are more ligands of the same category, they are named alphabetically.

5) Naming of prefixes: Sometimes a single molecule of the ligand contains the word di or tri etc. in its name, for e.g. ethylenediamine or trialkylphosphine. If two or more molecules of such ligands are present in the complex, then to avoid the repetition of the words di , tri etc., the prefixes in the greek language 'bis', 'tris', 'tetrakis' etc. are used before the names of ligand. For e.g.

$[Co(en)_2Cl_2]\ Cl$ dichlorobis-(ethylenediamine)cobalt(III) chloride.

6) Oxidation states: The oxidation state of the central atom is shown by roman numerals I, II, III or 0 in parentheses ( ) at the end of the name of the complex, without a space between the two. For a negative oxidation state a minus sign is used before the roman figure and zero is used for zero oxidation state.

  Na $[Co(CO)_4]$ sodium tetracarbonylcobaltate(-I)

  $K_4\ [Ni(CN)_4]$ potassium tetracyanonickeletate(0)

7) point of attachment: If a unidentate ligand has within itself more than one atom which can donate the electron pair it becomes necessary to show which atom is acting as donor , then the symbol of the donor atom is written after the name of the ligand with separation by hyphen. For e.g.

$(NH_3)_3\ [Cr(SCN)_6]$ ammonium hexathiocyanato-S-chromate(III)

    or ammonium isothiocyanatochromate(III)

8) Abbreviations: some ligand possess long and complicated names while naming such ligands their short forms are used in the formula as listed in table of ligands.

9) Bridging groups: Ligands that bridge two metal atoms in a polynuclear complex are preceded by the greek letter μ. It is repeated before the name of each kind of bridging group. The resulting complex is called a bridged ligand. Example:

Octaaquo- μ - dihydroxo diiron(III) sulphate

10) Geometrical isomerism: Geometrical isomerism are named by term cis to denote adjacent (90^0 away) positions and the term trans for opposite (180^0 away) positions. In addition it is essential to use a number system to show the position of each ligand. e.g. in case of square planar complexes groups 1-3 and 2-4 are in trans positions as shown below.

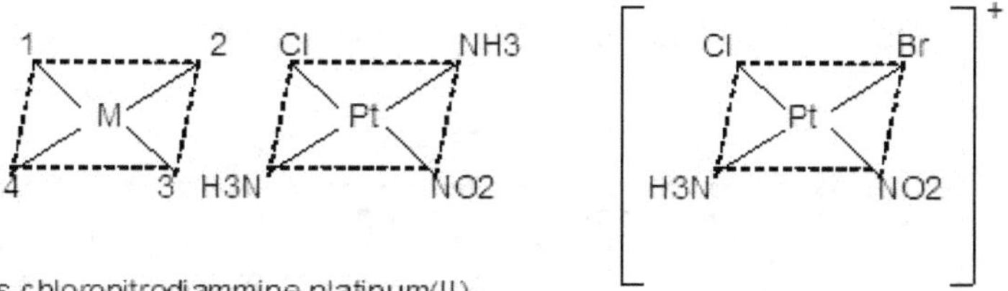

trans-chloronitrodiammine platinum(II)

1-chloro3nitrobromoammineplatinum(II)ion.

The number system for octahedral complexes has the trans positions numbered 1-6, 2-4 and 3-5.

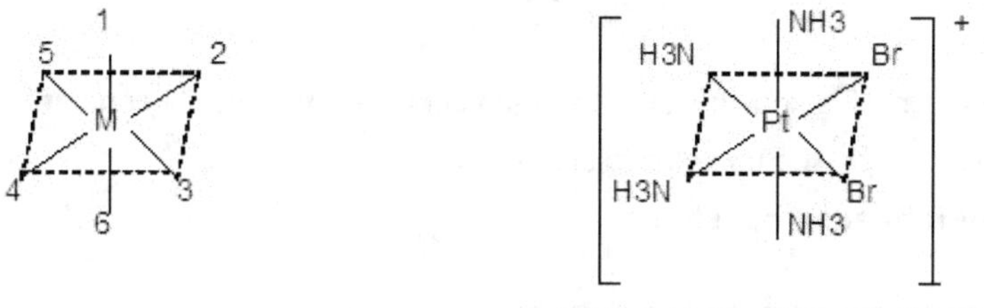

cis-dibromotetraamminerhodium(III) ion

11) Optical isomers: Dextro and laevo rotatory compounds are shown either by (+) or (-) signs or by letters d or l respectively.

1.5 Formation constants (Formation of complexes)

Equilibrium constant for Formation of complexes:

Many of the complex formation reactions take place in aqueous medium. Water sometimes itself acts as a ligand, hence first an aquo complex is formed. For example, when nickel sulphate is dissolved in water following reaction takes place,

$$NiSO_4 + 6\,H_2O \rightleftharpoons [Ni(H_2O)_6]\,SO_4$$

$$\text{an aquo complex}$$

Ammonia solution when added to the solution of this aquo complex, water molecules from the coordination sphere are replaced by ammonia molecule. Thus,

$$[Ni(H_2O)_6]^{2+} + 6\,NH_3 \rightleftharpoons [Ni(NH_3)_6]^{2+} + 6\,H2O$$

The equilibrium constant K, of the above reaction can be written as,

$$K = \frac{[Ni(NH3)_6]^{2+}\,[H2O]^6}{[Ni(H2O)_6]^{2+}\,[NH_3]^6} = 10^8$$

 As water is present in large excess the concentration of water is constant then we have,

$$K = \frac{[Ni(NH3)_6{}^{2+}]}{[Ni(H2O)_6{}^{2+}]\,[NH_3]^6} = 10^8$$

For such reaction, K is known as the formation constant or stability constant. If the value to K is high, the complex is stable.

1.6 Types of formation constants

Formation of a complex is an equilibrium process. It can described in terms of suitable expression for equilibrium constants. Following are different types of formation or stability constants.

(i) Stepwise stability constants (K1, K2, --------Kn)

The formation of complex in solution proceeds by stepwise addition of a ligand to the metal. We obtain the following expressions.

$$M + L \leftrightarrow ML \qquad K_1 = \frac{[ML]}{[M][L]}$$

$$ML + L \leftrightarrow ML_2 \qquad K_2 = \frac{[ML_2]}{[ML][L]}$$

$$ML_2 + L \leftrightarrow ML_3 \qquad K_3 = \frac{[ML_3]}{[ML_2][L]}$$

$$ML_{n-1} + L \leftrightarrow ML_n \qquad K_n = \frac{[ML_n]}{[ML_{n-1}][L]}$$

Where, $K_1, K_2, \text{-----} K_n$ are called stepwise stability constants or stepwise formation constants. The quantities in the bracket represent the activities of the enclosed species. A stability constant is a measure of extent of association. On the other hand, a dissociation constant is an instability constant, because it describes the dissociation of the substance, thus.

$$HX \leftrightarrow H^+ + X^- \qquad K = \frac{[H]^+ [X]^-}{[HX]}$$

(ii) Overall stability constant (β)

This is the second type of equilibrium constant. It is the product of the successive formation constants. The formation of the complex MLn may also be expressed as,

$$M + L \leftrightarrow ML \qquad \beta_1 = \frac{[ML]}{[M][L]}$$

$$M + 2L \leftrightarrow ML_2 \qquad \beta_2 = \frac{[ML_2]}{[M][L]^2}$$

$$M + 3L \leftrightarrow ML_3 \qquad \beta_3 = \frac{[ML_3]}{[M][L]^3}$$

$$M + nL \leftrightarrow ML_n \qquad \beta_n = \frac{[ML_n]}{[M][L]^n}$$

The higher the value of overall stability constant for a complex they must be related to each other. For example, consider the following expression.

$$\beta_3 = \frac{[ML_3]}{[M][L]^3}$$

on multiplying both numerator and denominator by [ML] [ML$_2$] and on rearranging we have,

$$\beta_3 = \frac{[ML_3]}{[M][L]^3} \times \frac{[ML][ML_2]}{[ML][ML_2]}$$

$$\beta_3 = \frac{[ML]}{[M][L]} \times \frac{[ML_2]}{[ML][L]} \times \cdots \times \frac{[ML_n]}{[ML_{n-1}][L]}$$

i.e. $\qquad \beta_3 = K_1 \times K_2 \times \cdots \times K_n$

Thus, we say that a complex is stable if the equilibrium constant describing its formation is large.

1.7 Factors affecting the stability of complex ions

The stability of complex ion largely depends on-

i) Nature of the central metal ion

ii) Nature of the ligand, and iii) chelation.

i) Nature of the central metal ion:

A metal ion is an electron acceptor and a ligand is an electron donor. The capacity of a metal ion to accept electrons and also to attract negatively charged ligands depends upon a) charge to radius ratio of the central metal ion and b) electronegativity of the metal ion.

a) Charge to radius ratio of the central metal ion:

The charge on the metal ion is equal to its oxidation state. Thus,

$$\text{Charge density} = \frac{\text{Charge on the metal ion}}{\text{Radius of the same ion}}$$

i.e. **greater the charge and smaller the size of the ion, greater is the stability of the complex.** For e.g. complexes formed by Fe^{3+} ion are more stable than Fe^{2+} ion. As the charge density on the metal ion increases, the stability of its complex also increases.

b) Electronegativity of the metal ion:

The higher the electronegativity of the metal ion, the greater is its attraction for ligands and hence greater is the stability of the complex formed by it. For e.g. the size of Fe^{3+} is smaller than Fe^{2+} ion. Hence Fe^{3+} is more electronegative than Fe^{2+} ion. As a result, complexes formed by Fe^{3+} ion are more stable than Fe^{2+} ion.

ii) Nature of the ligand: The stability of the complex depends on:

a) Basic character of the ligand:

As the basic character of a ligand increases, its stability to donate electron pair also increases and hence the complex formed becomes more stable, e.g. CO, CN^- etc. are strong bases and hence complexes formed by such ligands are more stable.

b) Size and charge of the ligand:

The smaller the size and greater the charge on the ligand, greater is its attraction towards the metal. The complexes formed by F^- ion are more stable than Cl^- ion.

iii) Chelation:

Polydentate ligands (i.e. chelating ligands) form more stable complexes, than monodentate ligands. The chelate complexes containing five and six membered rings are most stable. e.g. $[Ni(en)_3]^{2+}$ (where en= ethylenediamine) is much more stable than $[Ni(NH_3)_6]^{2+}$ ion. This is because ethylenediamine is a bidentate ligand and it forms a ring. The structures of these complexes are shown below.

Chelate complexes:

A chelating or multidentate ligand is a group that can attach to the same metal ion through more than one of its atoms. Chelating agents are known which can **attach to metal ions through two, three, four, five or even more donor atoms.** Out of these chelating agents those which can attach to the same metal ion through two of its atoms is the most common. Thus, chelating complexes are very stable. e.g. $[Cu(en)_2SO_4]$ is known as chelate compound, the cation $[Cu(en)_2]^{2+}$ is called a chelate ion and the ethylenediamine (en) is called a chelate ligand.

Complexes which exchange ligands rapidly are generally called 'labile complexes. On the other hand, complexes which exchange ligands at a slow rate are called **non-labile** or **inert complexes.**

1.8 Applications of coordinate compounds

Coordination compounds plays an important role in living beings and in the chemical industries. An example is chlorophyll- it is an important constituent of plant life, it is a co-ordination compound containing Mg(II). The red colour of blood is due to haemoglobin. It is a coordination compound containing Fe(II). Most of the elements present in trace amount in human body functions in the form of coordination compounds.

Coordination compounds play an important role in chemical industry as catalysts. Wilkinson's catalyst, Chlorotris(tri-phenylphosphine) - $RhCl(PPh_3)_3$ is used in the manufacture of alkane from alkene. Ziegler Natta catalyst based on titanium tetrachloride and diethyl aluminium chloride as co-catalyst can polymerize ethylene to high density ethylene (HDPE) at moderate to low temperature and standard pressure.

coordination compounds are also used in soil treatment, water softening, corrosion control etc. Complex compounds has many application in different fields. There are innumerable applications of coordination compounds in analytical chemistry, various industries and in biochemistry. Following are the some fields in which complex compound processes possesses important application. Some of the important applications are discussed below.

1.8.1 Analytical chemistry

a) Qualitative Analysis:

Coordination complex compounds were used in the identification of metal ion from the colour of the complex formed by that metal ion.

Example- The separation of Cd^{2+} from Cu^{2+} in group IIA is done by cyanide method. The method is based on comparative stability of the complexes $K_3[Cu(CN)_4]$ and $K_2[Cd(CN)_4]$. The copper complex is much more stable as compared to cadmium complex so when H_2S is passed through a solution containing Cd^{2+} and Cu^{2+} ions after treating the solution with CN- the cadmium alone gets precipitated where as Cu^{2+} remains in solution.

b) Quantitative Analysis

i) In Volumetric Analysis: Disodium salt of EDTA quantitatively react with Ca^{2+}, Mg^{2+} and many other cations. This reaction can be used for quantitative determination of these metal ions by titrating them against standard solution of EDTA using a Eriochrome black T as indicator. Volumetric determination of CN^- by Ag^+ in ammonical medium by using KI as indicator.

ii) In Gravimetric Analysis: For the precipitation of the metal ion or for the removal of interference of the metal ion coordinate complexes are used very effectively. In the estimation of nickel, nickel is treated with DMG, which forms

Ni[DMG] complex. From the complex amount of nickel is estimated.

iii) Spectrophotometric determination of trace elements of metal ions ; The many transition metal ions forms coloured compounds with coordinate complexes, which are detected by using spectrophotometric method. This method is used to detect the presence and estimate the amounts in trace amount. Fe(II) forms dark red complex with o-phenanthroline over a pH range 2 to 9.

iv) Solvent extraction: Chelates are mostly soluble in organic solvents than water. By taking this advantage of this fact it is possible to extract them into water immiscible organic phase. For example, Al^{3+} and Fe^{3+} for n complexes with oxime. Fe^{3+} oxime complex is easily soluble in chloroform and hence can be separated from Al^{3+} at pH 3 by addition of oxime.

1.8.2 Industrial Applications

Coordination complexes have very large applications in various types of industrial processes.

i) In water softening industry: The ion exchange resins, form complex compound with both cation and anion and removes them from the equation solution.

ii) In paint industry: Many coloured compounds are co-ordinate complex compounds.

iii) In drug industry: Many drugs are co-ordinate complexes

iv) In extraction of metal from ore: Silver and gold are extracted from their over due to the formation of their soluble cyanide complexes like $Ag[(CN)_3]^-$ and $Au[(CN)_2]^-$ respectively.

v) In photography: Silver halide forms $Ag[(S_2O_3)_2]^{3-}$ complex ion with $Na_2S_2O_3$, which is used to dissolve the unreacted silver halide.

vi) In electrochemistry: For the electroplating of metal. A number of metals are electroplated using a solution of their complex ions. For example Cu, Ag, Au were electroplated on the other metals or nonmetal material also by using this technique.

vii) Food Preservation: In food preservation coordination complexes are used.

1.8.3 Biological applications

Role of metal complexes in biochemistry is very large. The action of many enzymes depends on the presence of metal complexes in their structure. Haemoglobin in red blood cells contains an iron complex. Vitamin B_{12} is a cobalt complex. Chlorophyll in green plant contains Mg-porphyrin complex, etc.

CHAPTER 2: WERNERS THEORY

2.1 Werner's Coordination Theory

Werner, in 1893, at the age of 26, proposed his theory to explain the formation of compounds in which the number or bonds formed by the central metal atom is greater than that expected from the usual valency considerations. He introduced the concept of auxiliary valence. Some of compounds studied by him were $CoCl_3.6(NH_3)$, $Fe(CN)_2.4KCN$, $PtCl_4.6(NH_3)$ etc. for this work he was awarded a noble prize in chemistry in 1913.

2.2 Postulates of Werner's theory

Werner's theory includes the postulates.

1) Most of the metals show two types of valency.
    (a) Primary or ionisable valency (according to modern terminology it corresponds to oxidation number).
    (b) Secondary(auxiliary) or non-ionisable valency (according to modern terminology it corresponds to coordination number).
2) Every element tends to satisfy both its primary and secondary valencies. The Primary valencies of the element are satisfied by negative ions. Their attachment to metal ion is shown by the dotted lines (-----). The secondary valencies of the element are satisfied by negative ions or groups, or neutral molecules like H_2O, (NH_3) etc. or sometimes by positive ions. Their attachment to metal ion is shown by the thick lines (—). In each case

coordination number of the metal is fulfilled.

3) Every element possesses a fixed number of secondary valencies. This number is known as coordination number (CN). The coordination number shows the   number groups attached through coordinate bonds to the metal in a coordination   compound e.g. the CN of Cu(II) is 4 and that of Co(III) is 6 etc.

4) The coordinated groups are firmly held to the central atom while the other atoms are not firmly held. E.g. in the complex potassium ferrocyanide, $K_4[Fe(CN)_6]$,

5) the CN- ions are firmly held by iron. While K+ ions are not firmly held by iron.The secondary valencies are directed in definite directions in space, about the central atom or ion. The primary valencies on the other hand are non-directional.

The stereochemistry of complex is determined by the arrangement of such Groups (i.e. ligands) in space. For e.g. for metals with coordination No.4, the four secondary valencies are directed to the four corners of a tetrahedron or at the four corners of square. In table 2.1 complete series of $CoCl_3$ and NH_3 complexes are given.

Table 2.1: $CoCl_3$ and NH_3 complexes explaining Werner's theory

Complex	No. of Cl- ion ppted.	No. of ions shown by conductance	Modern formulation
$CoCl_3.6NH_3$	3	4	$[Co(NH_3)_6]^{3+}$, 3Cl-
$CoCl_3.5NH_3$	2	3	$[Co(NH_3)_5Cl]^{2+}$, 2Cl-
$CoCl_3.4NH_3$	1	2	$[Co(NH_3)_4Cl_2]^{+}$, Cl-
$CoCl_3.3NH_3$	0	1	$[Co(NH_3)_3Cl_3]$

The properties of these complexes can be explained on the basis of werner's postulates. In all these complexes the central metal ion, cobalt, shows secondary valency of six. The primary valency or oxidation state of the metal ions is three. Each structure may be so drawn that they satisfy both primary and secondary valence. It may also explain the observable properties.

The first compound $CoCl_3 \cdot 6NH_3$ may be written as $[Co(NH_3)_6]Cl_3$. Its structure may be shown as in figure 2.1. As there six ammonia molecules in the complex, they saturate the secondary valence. They are directly attached to the central cobalt atom. They are shown by thick lines. The primary valency is satisfied by three Cl^- ions. Since the CN of cobalt is six, there can only six groups (ligands) directly attached to it and these are occupied by NH3 molecules.

The Cl^- ions are not directly attached to cobalt and that is why they are shown by dotted lines. They are kept outside the coordination sphere. The combining power of a metal is divided into two spheres of attraction, the "inner" or "coordination sphere" and the "outer" or "ionization sphere". To distinguish the two spheres of attraction, Werner enclosed the inner or coordination sphere in a square bracket [ ].

The ligands that are directly attached to the central metal ion in a complex are said to be in coordination sphere or first sphere of attraction of the complex. The outer or ionization sphere contains the loosely held ionisable ion. As all the three Cl^- ions are loosely bond to the central cobalt atom (shown by dashed lines), they ionize and hence are immediately precipitated as AgCl on the addition of $AgNO_3$. The number of ions obtainable from each molecule is four i.e. one $[Co(NH_3)_6]$ ion and $3Cl^-$ ions which are agreement with experimental observation.

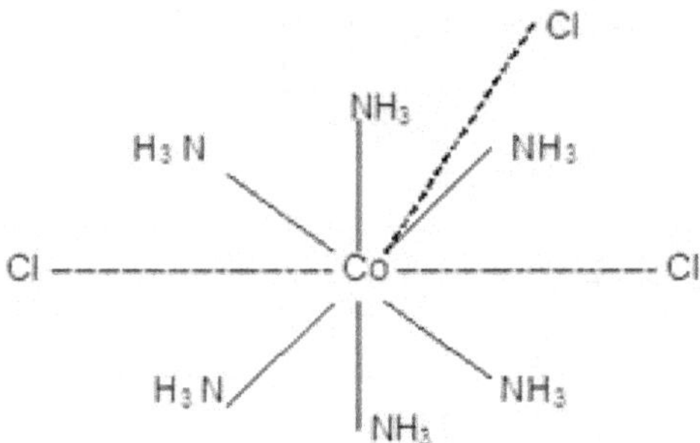

Figure 2.1: $CoCl_3 \cdot 6NH_3$ showing primary (dotted lines) and secondary valencies (thick lines) satisfied in Coordination complex

The second compound viz. $CoCl_3 \cdot 5NH_3$ may be written as $[Co(NH_3)_5Cl]Cl_2$. Its structure may be shown as in figure 2.2. As there five ammonia molecules in the complex, one Cl⁻ ions will have to play a dual role of the satisfying both the primary and secondary valence. This Cl⁻ ion is shown both by thick as well as dotted line in the diagram. The Cl⁻ ion directly attached to the cobalt atom. It is different from the other two Cl⁻ ions. It is inside the coordination sphere. It is said to be in the first coordination sphere. It is non ionizable. Hence it is not precipitated by $AgNO_3$.

The other two Cl⁻ ion are not directly attached to cobalt and that is why they are shown by dotted lines. They are kept outside the coordination sphere. They are ionizable. They are precipitated by $AgNO_3$. The number of ions obtainable from each molecule is three i.e. one $[Co(NH_3)_5Cl]^{2+}$ ion and $2Cl^-$ ions which are agreement with experimental observation.

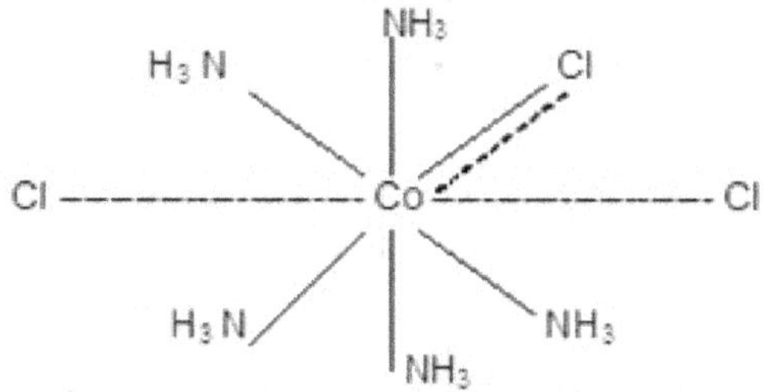

Figure 2.2: $CoCl_3$. $5NH_3$ showing primary (dotted lines) and secondary valencies (thick lines) satisfied in Coordination complex

On the other hand, the compounds $CoCl_3.4NH_3$ and $CoCl_3.3NH_3$ respectively may be formulated as $[Co(NH_3)_4Cl_2]$ Cl and $[Co(NH_3)_3Cl_3]$ respectively their structures shown in figure 2.3 and 2.4. Figure 2.3 shows only one Cl- ions which is ionizable. It is precipitated by AgNO3. It remains outside the square bracket. The number of ions shall be only two i.e. one $[Co(NH_3)_4Cl_2]^+$, and one Cl⁻ ion. Figure 2.4 shows no ionizable Cl- ions. All the three Cl- ions remain inside the square bracket. The compounds behave as a non-electrolyte.

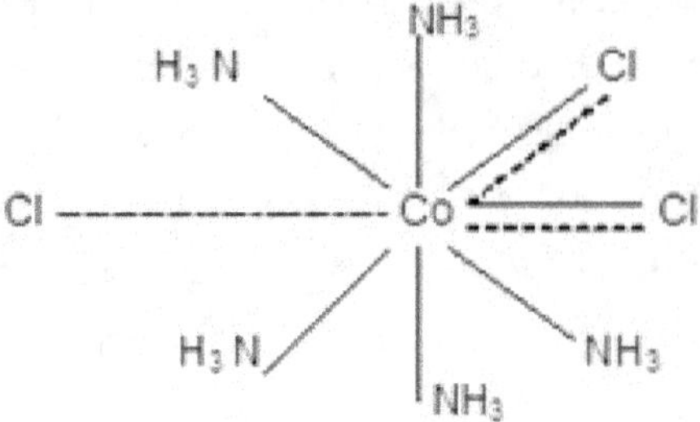

Figure 2.3: CoCl$_3$. 4NH$_3$ showing primary (dotted lines) and secondary valencies (thick lines) satisfied in Coordination complex

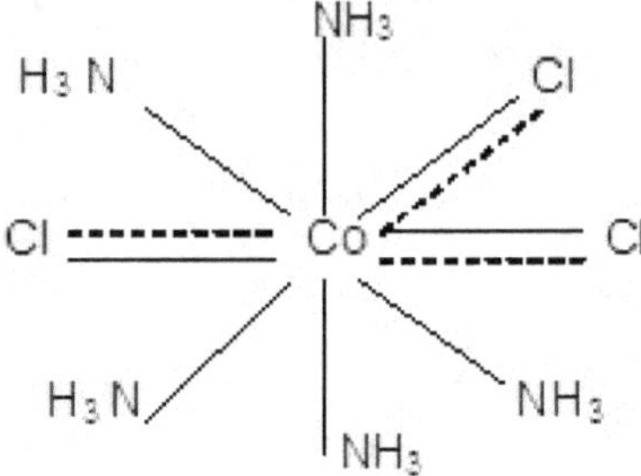

Figure 2.4: CoCl$_3$. 3NH$_3$ showing primary (dotted lines) and secondary valencies (thick lines) satisfied in Coordination complex

Structure Werner confirmed the number of primary and secondary valence of the metal ion in the given complex by physical and chemical methods. He used molar conductance values to determine the number of ions per molecules, thus assuming groups to the first coordination sphere. Chemical methods like ppt. of Cl- ions by AgNO$_3$ to determine the number of ionizable Cl- ions per molecule were also used.

2.3 The comparison of ions in two coordination spheres

[Co(NH$_3$)$_6$]	Cl$_3$
(i) They are in the first coordination sphere.	(i) They are in the second coordination sphere.
(ii) They are shown inside the square bracket.	(ii) They are shown outside the square bracket.
(iii) They represent secondary valence.	(iii) They represent primary valence.
(iv) They are non-ionisable.	(iv) They are ionisable.
(v) They are directly bonded to the central atom.	(v) They are not directly bonded to the central atom.

2.4 Charge on a complex ion

The charge on the complex ion depends on the nature of the coordinated ligands or groups attached to the central metal atom. The complex is a charged species having positive or negative charge which is formed by the union of a simple metal with one or more neutral molecules or one or more anions. For e.g. [Co^{III} (NH$_3$)$_5$Cl]$^{2+}$ ion is formed by the union of five ammonia molecules and one chloride ion with one Co^{3+} ion. A complex ion possesses a net +2 charge, which is the algebraic sum of the charges carried by the central metal ion and the ligands attached to it. For e.g. the charge on the above complex is +2, because the cobalt ion carries +3 charge, ammonia molecule is neutral and one chloride ion possesses −1 charge

i.e. (+3) + (0) + (-) = 3+ 0 - 1 = +2 charge.

CHAPTER 3: ISOMERISM IN COORDINATION COMPLEXES

Definition of Isomerism:

somerism are defined as substances, Molecules or ions with same chemical formulae but having different structures, and the phenomenon is called as isomerism.

3.1 Types of Isomerism in Coordination Complexes

Coordination complexes are classified into mainly two groups i) Structural Isomerism and ii) Stereoisomerism

Structural isomerism	**Stereoisomerism**
i) Ionization isomerism	i) Geometrical isomerism
ii) Ligand isomerism	or cis- trans isomerism
iii) Linkage isomerism	or position isomerism
iv) Coordination isomerism	
v) Coordination Position isomerism	ii) Optical isomerism or mirror image Isomerism

3.2 Structural isomerism

structural isomerism is due to different possible arrangements of atoms or groups in their complexes they have different ligands within their coordination sphere. Structural isomerism may be of different types as shown below.,

3.2.1 Ionization isomerism

Structural isomerism is due to different possible arrangements of atoms or groups in their molecules. Ionization isomerism name is used to describe isomers that give different ions in solution. The composition of these isomers is the same. e.g.

$[Co(H_2O)_5Br]\ SO_4$ bromopentaaquocobalt(III) sulphate

It gives SO_4^{2-} ion in solution & can be precipitated with $BaCl_2$.

$[Co(H_2O)_5SO_4]\ Br$ sulphatopentaaquocobalt (III) bromide

It gives Br^- ion in solution & can be precipitated with $AgNO_3$

Other examples of ionization isomerism.

$[Co(NH_3)_4Cl_2]\ NO_2$ & $[Co(NH_3)_4Cl\ NO_2]\ Cl$

$[Pt(NH_3)_4Cl_2]\ Br_2$ & $[Pt(NH_3)_4\ Br_2]\ Cl_2$

$[Pt(NH_3)_3\ Br]NO_2$ & $[Pt(NH_3)_3NO_2]\ Br$

$[Co(en)_2(NCS)_2]\ Cl$ & $[Co(en)_2(NCS)\ Cl]\ (NCS)$

3.2.2 Hydrate isomerism

This type of isomerism is similar to ionization isomerism, in this replacement of a coordinated group by water of hydration is formed. e.g. there are three isomers of CrCl3. $6H_2O$ as

$[Cr(H_2O)_6]Cl_3$ All the Cl- ions are outside the square bracket and precipitated by $AgNO_3$ as AgCl.

$[Cr(H_2O)_5\ Cl]\ Cl_2.\ H_2O$ Only two Cl- ions are outside the square bracket and precipitated by $AgNO_3$ as AgCl.

$[Cr(H_2O)_4\ Cl_2]\ Cl.\ 2H_2O$ Only one Cl- ion is outside the square bracket and precipitated by $AgNO_3$ as AgCl.

Some other examples of hydrate isomerism are

$[Co(en)_2(H_2O)(Cl)]\,Cl_2$ & $[Co(en)_2\,Cl_2]\,Cl.H_2O$

$[Co(Py)_2(H_2O)_2Cl_2]Cl$ & $[Co(Py)_2(H_2O)\,Cl_3]\,H_2O$

$[Co(NH_3)_4(H_2O)\,Cl]\,Cl_2$ & $[Co(NH_3)_4Cl_2]Cl.H_2O$

3.2.3 Ligand Isomerism

Certain ligands themselves can exist in isomeric forms. e.g. diaminopropane can exist with 1,2 diaminopropane (pn) and 1,3 diaminopropane (tn). Thus, the ligands (pn) & (tn) when associated into complexes, the corresponding complexes are isomers of each other. Hence $[CO(pn)_2Cl_2]^+$ & $[Co(tn)_2Cl_2]^+$ ion ligand isomers of each other.

$$1 \quad 2 \quad 3$$

$$CH_3-CH_2-CH_2 \qquad H_2C-CH-CH_3 \qquad H_2C-CH_2-CH_3$$

Propane
$$\qquad\qquad\qquad\quad |\ \ | \qquad\qquad\quad |\qquad\quad |$$

$$NH_2\ NH_2 \qquad\quad NH_2 \qquad NH_2$$

1,2 diaminopropane
(pn)

1,3 diaminopropane
or trimethylene diamine
(tn)

3.2.4 Linkage isomerism

This type of isomerism is formed when monodentate ligand has two different atoms available for coordination. The linkage between the metal and ligand in one isomer is through one ligand atom and of its isomer is through another. The best known ligand of this type are NO_2^-, SCN^-, $S_2O_3^{-2}$ ions.

For e. g. NO_2^- ion in Cobalt (III) complexes can be attached either through nitrogen as Co- NO_2 or through oxygen as Co- ONO (Nitrito) thus,

$[(NH_3)_5Co-NO_2]Cl_2$ & $[(NH_3)_5Co-ONO]Cl_2$

nitropentaamminecobalt(III) chloride   nitritopentaamminecobalt (III) chloride

some other examples are

$[(NH_3)_2(py)_2Co-(NO_2)_2]NO_3$ & $[(NH_3)_2(py)_2Co-(ONO)_2]NO_3$

$[(NH_3)_5\,Ir-(NO_2)]Cl_2$ & $[(NH_3)_5\,Ir-(ONO)]Cl_2$

In the above examples all ligands other than nitro are written to the left of the metal in order to stress how the nitrate ion is bound to the metal.

some other examples are

$M - NCS$ Metal isothiocyanate complex

e.g. $NH_4[Cr(NH_3)_2 (NCS)_4]$

ammonium tetraisothiocyanatodiamminechromate (III)

$M - SCN$ Metal thiocyanate complex

e.g. $(NH_4)_2 [Pt (SCN)_6]$

ammonium hexathiocyanatoplatinate(IV)

$M - S_2O_3$ metal thiosulphato – s

e.g. $Na_3[Ag(S_2O_3)_2]$ sodium bis(thiosulphato)argentate(I)

$M - OS_2O_2$ metal thiosulphato – O

3.2.5 Coordination isomerism

Complexes containing both cationic and anionic species results in coordination isomerism due to the interchange of metals.

e.g. $[Co(NH_3)_6]$ $[Cr(CN)_6]$ & $[Cr(NH_3)_6]$ $[Co(CN)_6]$

$[Co(NH_3)_6]$ $[Cr(C_2O_4)_3]$ & $[Cr(NH_3)_6]$ $[Co(C_2O_4)_3]$

This type of isomerism is also shown by compounds which contain the same metal ion both in the cationic and anionic species. e.g.

$[Pt^{II}(NH_3)_4] [Pt^{IV} Cl_4]$ & $[Pt^{IV}(NH_3)_4] [Pt^{II} Cl_4]$

3.2.6 Coordination position isomerism

This is a special type of coordination isomerism. It is shown by bridged complexes. It involves different attachment of ligands. e.g.

$$[(NH_3)_4\ Co \underset{OH}{\overset{OH}{\diagup\!\!\!\diagdown}} Co\ (NH_3)_2\ Cl_2]SO_4$$

Trans- Dichlorohexaammine-μ- dihydroxodicobalt(III) sulphate
Unsymmetrical

and

$$[Cl\,(NH_3)_3\,Co\underset{\displaystyle OH}{\overset{\displaystyle OH}{<}}\!\!\!\!\!> Co\,(NH_3)_3\,Cl\,]SO_4$$

Cis- Dichlorohexaammine-μ- dihydroxodicobalt(III) sulphate
Symmetrical

3.3 Stereoisomerism or Space Isomerism

Two complex compounds containing same ligands which are coordinated to the same central metal ion but when the arrangement of ligands in space is different than such complex compounds are called stereoisomers of each other. It is of two types:

1) Geometrical isomerism or cis- trans isomerism or position isomerism
2) Optical isomerism or   Mirror image Isomerism

3.3.1 Geometrical isomerism or cis- trans isomerism or position isomerism

This isomerism is shown by complexes in which either the same two ligands occupy adjacent positions to each other (Latin, cis- same) or opposite to each other (Latin, trans - across).   Therefore this isomerism is not possible with compounds having C.N. 2,3 and for tetrahedral complexes with C.N. 4 . For tetrahedral complexes all the four positions are adjacent to each other. This isomerism is possible only in four coordinate square planar complexes and six coordinate octahedral complexes.

3.3.2 Geometrical isomerism in square planar complexes

Geometrical isomerism shown by square planar complexes is of following types:

a) **[MA$_2$X$_2$] type**: Here is M is the central metal ion and A and X are the two monodentate ligands, e.g. [Pt(NH$_3$)$_2$Cl$_2$] complex. It exists in two forms. viz. cis and trans forms.

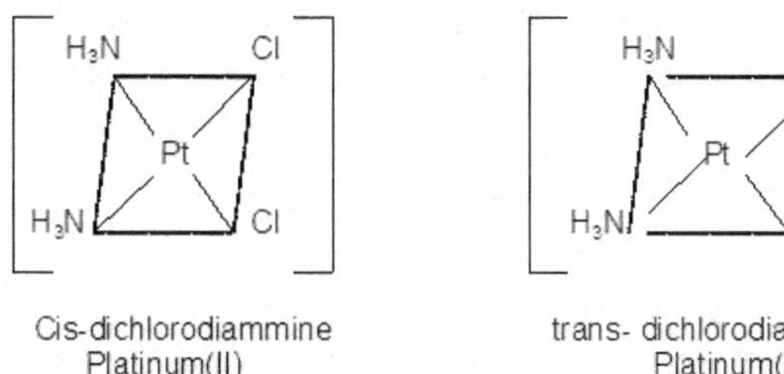

Cis-dichlorodiammine
Platinum(II)

trans- dichlorodiammine
Platinum(II)

b) [MA₂XY] type: Here is M is the central metal ion usually Pt and A is the neutral ligand such as NH3, Pyridine etc. and X and Y are anionic ligands like Cl^-, Br^-, I^-, SCN^-, NO_2^-.

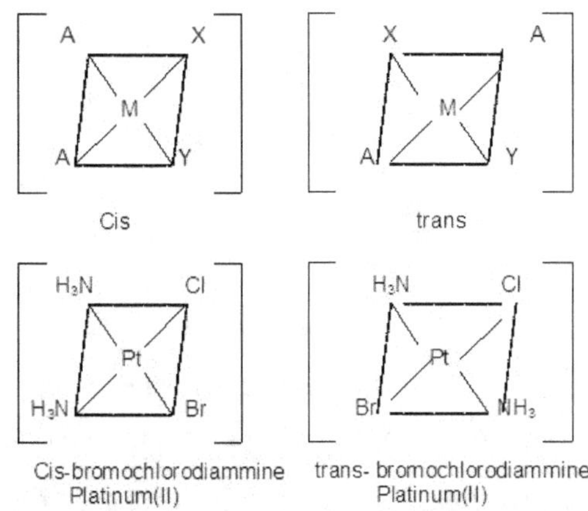

Cis

trans

Cis-bromochlorodiammine
Platinum(II)

trans- bromochlorodiammine
Platinum(II)

(C) [MABCD] Type: Complexes of this type shall exhibit three isomers. We can write three

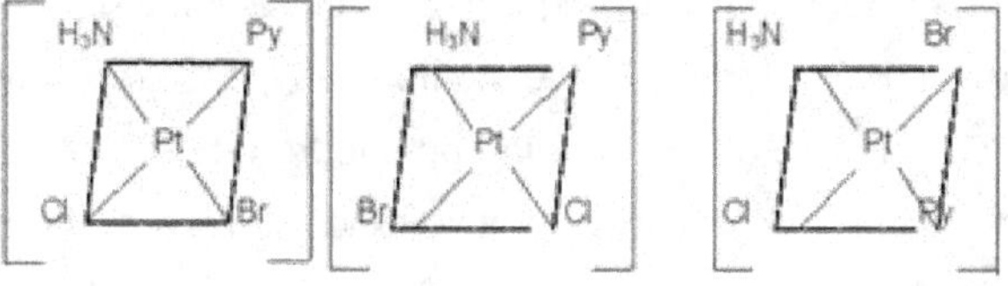

structures by fixing any one of the ligands for e.g. A at one position and then placing ligands B, C or D trans to it. Three isomers of the complex [Pt (NH₃) (Py) (Cl) (Br)] have actually been isolated corresponding to NH₃ trans to each of the remaining three ligands.

(d) Geometrical isomers are also found for square planar complexes which have

29

unsymmetrical bidentate ligands, e.g. the compound [Pt(gly)2] where (gly= glycinato) shows both cis-and trans isomers.

(e) Geometrical isomerism is also shown by bridged binuclear planner complexes of the type $M_2A_2X_4$ e.g. [Pt Cl_2 PEt_3]$_2$

Note: Complexes of the type MA4, MA3B, MAB3 have no geometrical isomers because, every possible arrangement for any of these complexes will be exactly the same.

3.3.3 Geometrical isomerism in octahedral complexes

Many complexes with C.N.6 is known and they are well studied. In these omplexes the six ligands are arranged around the central metal ion, at the corners of regular octahedron. These complexes possess regular octahedral structures as shown in fig. A regular octahedron has eight faces and six equivalent vertices. In an octahedral complex the metal is at the center and the ligands are placed at the vertices. The positions in the octahedron are usually numbered as follows.

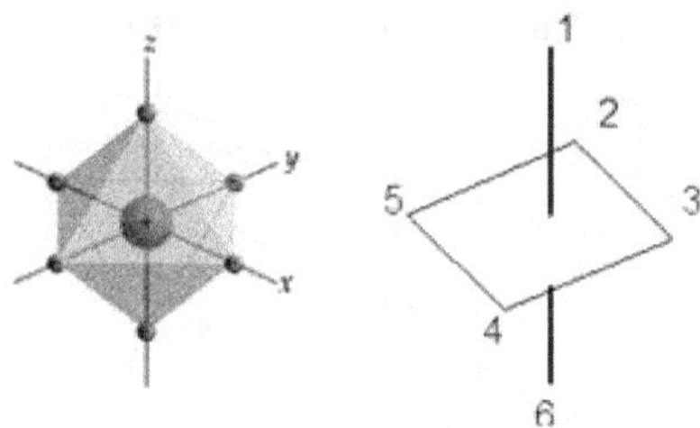

Types of octahedral complexes:

(1) Octahedral complexes containing only monodentate ligands.

(2) Octahedral complexes containing monodentate and symmetrical bidentate chelating ligands.

(3) Octahedral complexes containing unsymmetrical chelating ligands.

3.3.3.1 Octahedral complexes containing only monodentate ligands

(i) MA$_4$X$_2$ type: They possess two isomers in which cis-isomer has two X's at adjacent positions and in trans isomer two X's at opposite positions, e.g. $[Co(NH_3)_4Cl_2]^+$

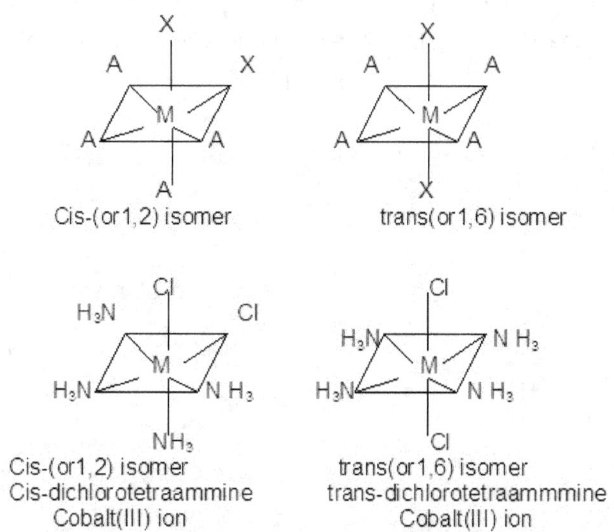

(ii) [MA$_3$X$_3$] type: The complexes of this type are also known to gives cis- and trans isomers, e.g. [Co(NH$_3$)$_3$Cl$_3$] cis –isomer is obtained when all the like groups occupy the positions on the same face of an octahedron (1,2,3 and 4,5,6 positions), i.e. facial isomer and in trans-isomer three positions are arranged that two are opposite to each other i.e. meridional isomer.

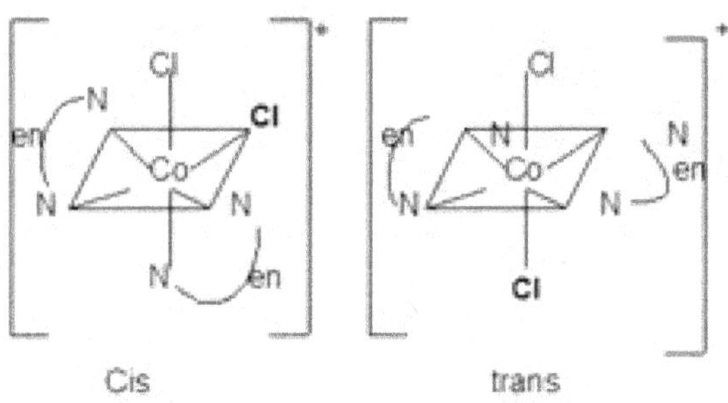

Cis-(or1,2) isomer   trans(or1,6) isomer

(iii) [M(ABCDEF)] Type: In this type all the six ligands are monodentate and different. Theoretically 15 different isomers should be possible. Practically three isomers of the complex [Pt (Py) (NH3) (NO2) (Cl) (Br) (I)] have been separated.

3.3.3.2 Octahedral complexes containing monodentate and symmetrical bidentate chelating ligands

(i) [M(A-A) $_2$ X$_2$] type: Here (A-A) is symmetrical bidentate chelating ligands in which the two letteres A and A indicate the two similar coordinating atoms, e.g. ethylenediamine (NH_2-CH_2-CH_2-NH_2). X is an anionic monodentate ligand such as Cl-, CN-, NO^{2-} etc. for e.g. [Co(en)$_2$ Cl$_2$]+ ion. It exists in cis and trans isomeric forms.

Cis   trans

Cis and trans isomers of [Co(en) $_2$ (Cl)$_2$]+

(ii) [M(A-A)2 XY] type: This type of complex contains two symmetrical bidentae ligands X and Y. for e.g. [Co(en) $_2$ (Cl) (Br)]+. This complex cation exists in cis and trans isomeric forms.

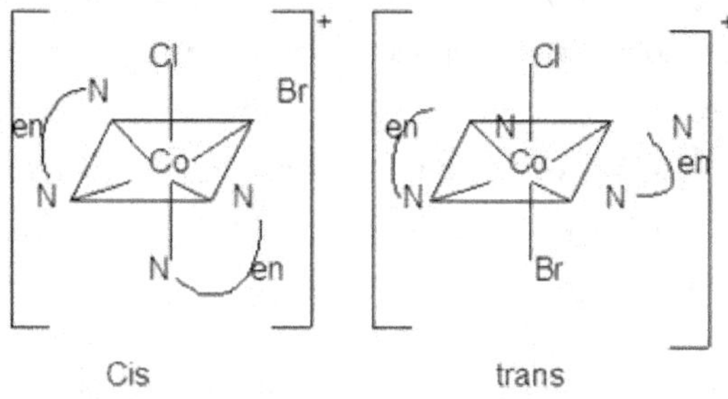

Cis   trans

Cis and trans isomers of [Co(en)$_2$ (Cl) (Br)]+

3.3.3.3 Octahedral complexes containing unsymmetrical chelating ligands

(i) [M(AB)$_3$ type :

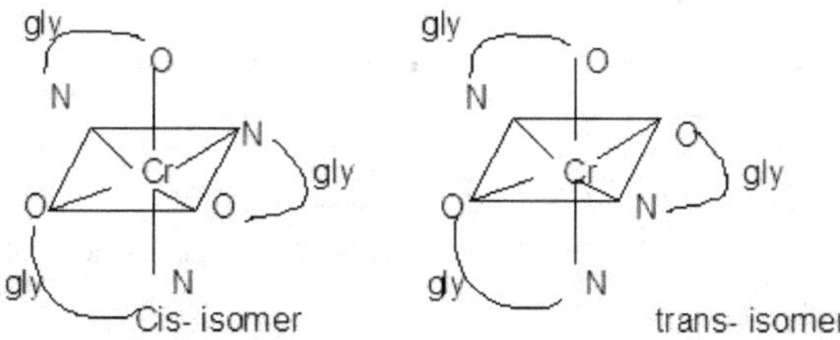

Cis- isomer   trans- isomer

Here AB is an unsymmetrical bidentate ligand in which the two letters A and B indicate the two different coordinating atoms. Complexes of this type exist in cis and trans isomers. For e.g. cis and trans [Cr(gly)$_3$].

3.3.4 Optical or mirror image isomerism

Optical isomerism is due to molecular asymmetry. Optical isomerism is common in octahedral complexes containing bidentate ligands. it is crucial to know the meaning of some of the terms related to optical activity

3.3.4.1 Optical Activity

The property of a complex to rotate the plane of polarized light passing through it is called its optical activity and the complex possessing this property or power is said to be optically active

Optically active complexes are said to exist in the two forms

33

a) **Dextrorotatory or d form**: One which rotate the plane of polarised light towards right it means in clockwise direction is called as dextrorotatory or d form.

b) **Laevo rotatory or l form**: One which rotate the plane of polarised light towards left means in anticlockwise direction is called levorotatory or l form.

d and l isomers are just mirror images of one another just as of left hand is the mirror image of the right hand. The d and l isomers are also termed as enantiomorphs (opposite forms) of one another. They have identical chemical and physical properties and differ only in direction in which they rotate the plane of polarized light.

3.3.4.2 Definition of optical isomerism

Two compounds having similar formula but possessing such an arrangement of groups or atoms in space around the metal ion that one structure is the mirror image of the other and these are not superimposable, are called optical isomers. The phenomenon is also called as enantiomorphism and two compounds are called as enantiomorphs.

3.3.4.3 Optical isomerism in square planar complexes

Very few square planar complexes show optical isomerism. This is because in a square planar complex, all the ligands and the metal ion lie in the same plane, and hence it possesses a plane or a center of symmetry. Square planar complexes do not show optical isomerism even if all the ligands are different. One such square planar complex,

Isobutylene diamine-meso-stilbenediamineplatinum(II) chloride has however, been resolved into two optical forms. Following structure shows that the complex has no plane or axis of symmetry and hence it is unsymmetrical and optically active.

e.g. $[Pt\ NH_2.CH(C_6H_5).CH(C_6H_5)NH_2.(NH_2CH_2.C(CH_3)_2.NH_2]\ Cl_2$

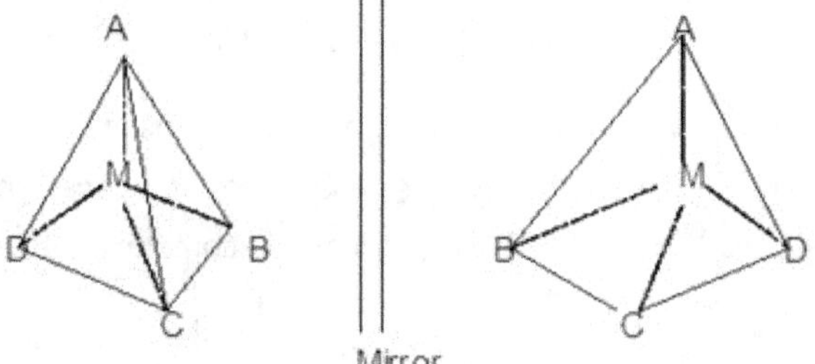

Optically active square planar complex

3.3.4.4 Optical isomerism in tetrahedral complexes

i) A tetrahedral complex of the type [MABCD]

e.g. [As(C$_2$H$_5$) (CH$_3$) (C$_6$H$_4$COO-) (S)] occurs at two optical isomers as shown in figure.

ii) Tetrahedral complex containing symmetrical bidentate ligands of the type M(A-A)$_2$ are not optically active, since they possess mirror- plane of symmetry.

iii) The tetrahedral complexes which have been shown to be optically active are those which contain unsymmetrical bidentate ligands.

Two optical isomers of a tetrahedral complex of [MABCD] type

The general formula of these complexes is [M(A-B)]. Tetrahedral complexes of Be(II), B(III) and Zn(II) with unsymmetrical bidentate ligands have been made and resolved. e.g. i)   bis-(benzoyl pyruvato) beryllium(II) & ii) bis-(benzoylacetonato)beryllium(II). The non super imposable mirror images of bis-(benzoylacetonato)beryllium(II) are shown in figure.

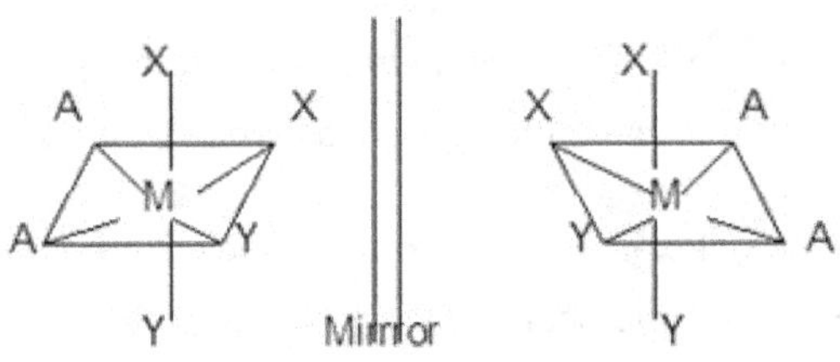

Mirror image isomers of bis(benzoyl-acetonato) beryllium(II)

3.3.4.5 Optical isomerism in Octahedral complexes

3.3.4.5.1 Octahedral complexes containing only monodentate ligands

a) [MA$_2$X$_2$Y$_2$] type: Complexes have two optical isomers as shown in fig.

e.g. [Pt(NH$_3$)$_2$ (Py)$_2$Cl$_2$]$^{2+}$

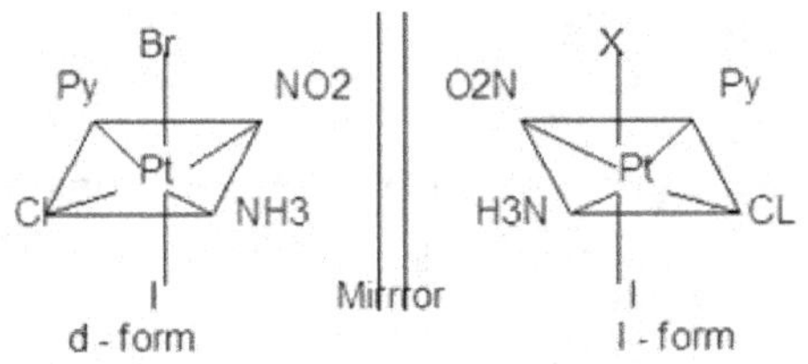

Mirror images of [MA$_2$X$_2$Y$_2$]

b) [MABCDEF] type: Complex of this type theoretically possesses 15 geometrical isomers. Each of these isomer possesses two optical isomers. E.g. [Pt(NH$_3$) (Py) (NO$_2$) (Cl) (Br) (I)]. For one form of this complex, the two optical isomers are shown in fig.

Mirror images of [Pt(NH$_3$) (Py) (NO$_2$) (Cl) (Br) (I)]

3.3.4.5.2 Octahedral complexes containing only symmetrical bidentate ligands

a) [M (A-A)$_3$ type complexes: This isomer possesses two optical isomers.

e.g. $[Co(en)_3]^{4+}$, $[Pt(en)_3]^{4+}$, $[Cr(C_2O_4)_3]^{3-}$ The optical isomers of $[Co(en)_3]$ are shown in figure

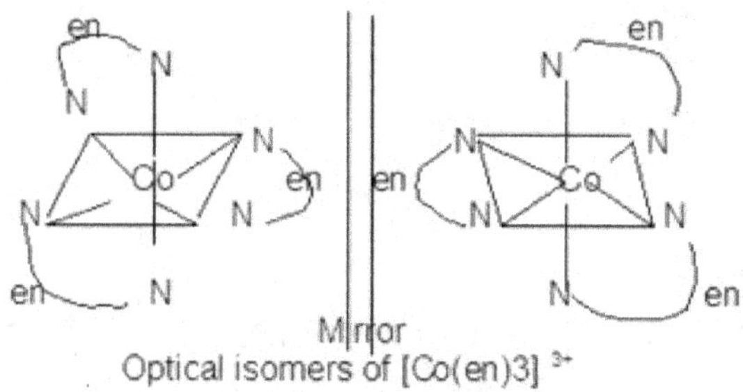

Optical isomers of $[Co(en)3]^{3+}$

b) [M (A-A)$_2$ (B-B) type complexes: Here A-A and B-B are symmetrical bidentate ligands. e.g. $[Co(en)_2 (C_2O_4)]^+$, it shows two optical isomers.

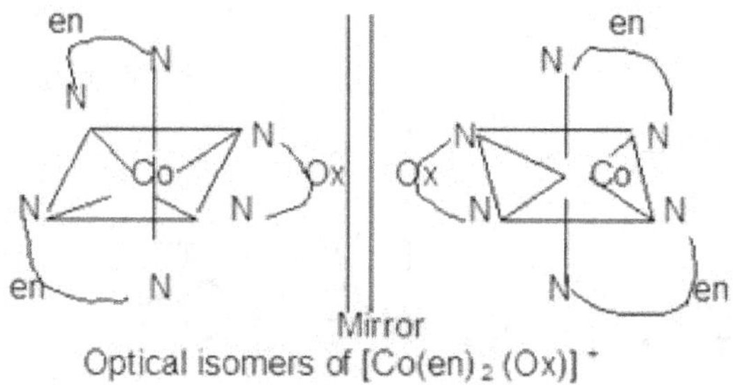

Optical isomers of $[Co(en)_2 (Ox)]^-$

3.3.4.5.3 Octahedral complexes containing monodentate & symmetrical bidentate ligands

a) [M(AA)$_2$X$_2$] type complexes. e.g. $[Co(en)_2 Cl_2]^+$ ion shows two optical isomers

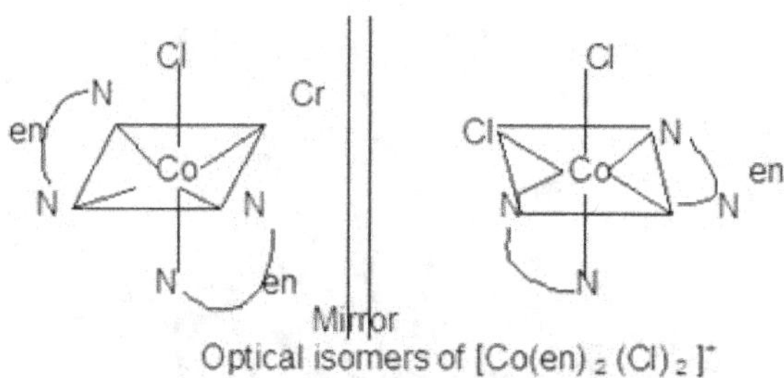

Optical isomers of $[Co(en)_2 (Cl)_2]^-$

b) [M(AA)$_2$ XY] type complexes: e.g. $[Co(en)_2 (NH_3) (Cl)]^{2+}$

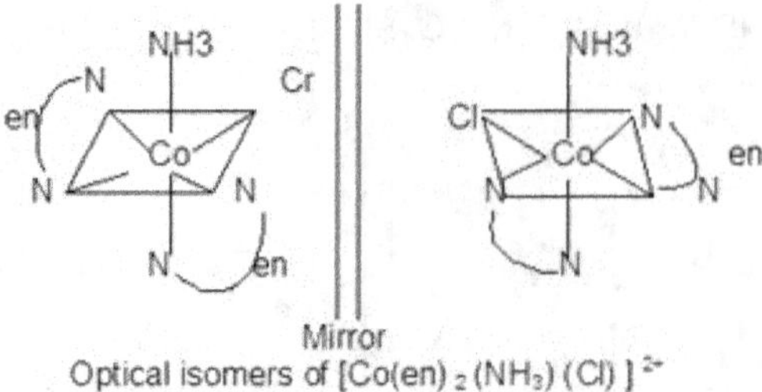

Mirror

Optical isomers of [Co(en) $_2$ (NH$_3$) (Cl)]$^{2+}$

3.3.4.5.4 Octahedral complexes containing optically active bidentate unsymmetrical bidentate ligands

The complexes of this type is [(Co(en)(Py)(NO$_2$)$_2$]$^+$ (where en= ethylenediamine, pn= 1,2-propane diamine), only the cis form of this compound, shows optical isomerism as

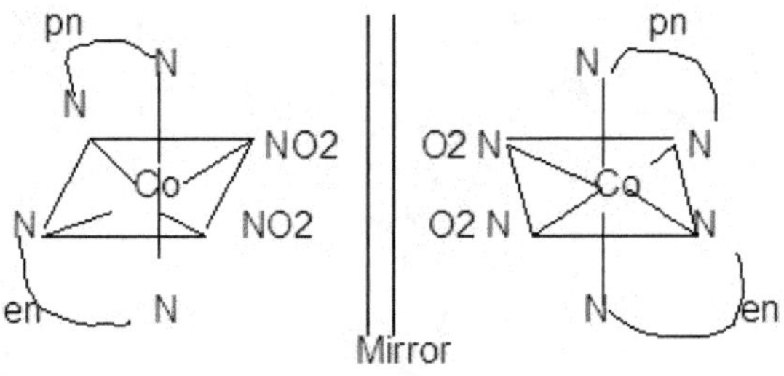

Mirror

38

CHAPTER 4: SIDGWICK THEORY

4.1 Electronic interpretation of Werner's Coordination Theory

Sidgwick interpreted Werner's coordination theory in terms of the electronic theory of valency of the atom. He extended the Lewis theory to bonding in coordination compounds. Sidgwick model was based on the following points.

i) Werner's primary valency is the electrovalency (positive valency) e.g. Cr^{+3} in $CrCl_3$. it arises due to the loss of electrons from the metal atom.

ii) Werner's secondary valency is the coordinate covalency (electron pair sharing). He suggested that, ligand acts as donor and metal ion as the acceptor of the electron pair. Thus in this type of valency a formation of coordinate bond takes place between the central metal ion and ligands, which is shown as L $\rightarrow$ M. thus according to Sidgwick idea, the structure of the complex $[Ni(NH_3)]^{2+}$ is shown in figure 4.1

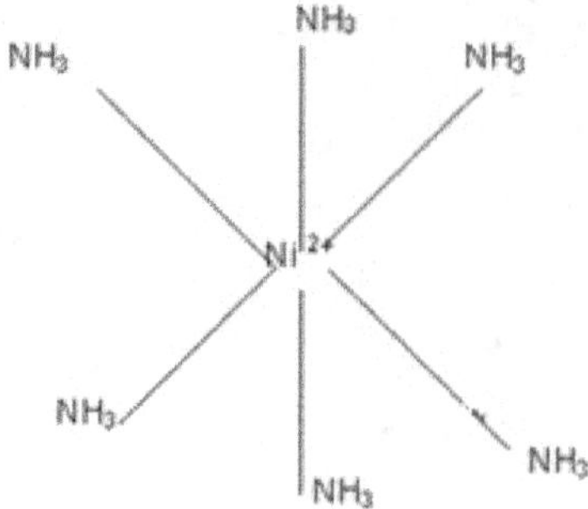

Figure 4.1: Structure of [Ni(NH$_3$)]$^{2+}$ ion complex

The formation six coordinate bonds between Ni^{2+} And six NH_3 molecules takes place by the donation of an electron pair from each NH_3 molecules to the central metal nickel ion, as shown by arrow. The number of bonds formed is equal to the C.N. of the metal ion. In this process of complex formation many metal ions achieve the stable configuration of nearest inert gas.

4.2 Sidgwick Concept of Effective Atomic Number

Sidgwick introduced the concept of effective atomic number (EAN) or inert gas rule so as to explain the tendency of different metal ions to form stable complexes. He suggested that metal ions will tend to accept electron pairs from donors until they achieve an inert gas configuration or effective atomic number of the next inert gas. One of the basic ideas of the electronic theory of valency is that one atom combines with the other because of its tendency to achieve a stable electronic configuration or the effective atomic number of next inert gas. This stable electronic configuration is usually identical with that of some gas. The metal ion achieves stable inert gas configuration by accepting electrons from the ligands. The stability of complex was assumed to be due to inert gas configuration of the metal ion. Thus, the process of coordination provides the metal atoms (ions) an opportunity to achieve stable configuration or the effective atomic number of an inert gas.

The effective atomic number (EAN) of a metal ion is calculated by subtracting the number of electrons lost in ion formation from the atomic number of the metal and then adding the number of electrons gained from the ligands, e.g. $[Co(NH_3)]^{3+}$ ion.

Number of electrons in Co (Z = 27)	= 27
Number of electrons in Co^{3+} ion formation	= 24
Number of electrons donated by the six NH_3 ligands (6x2)	= 12
$\therefore$ Total number of electrons associated with Co^{3+} in the complex	= 36
	= EAN = At No. of

Kr.Thus EAN of metal ion may be defined as the total number of electrons present in the valency shell of it including those gained by binding in the complex ion. THE EAN of various coordinate complexes are shown in table 4.1 and 4.2.

Table 4.1: Complexes obeying EAN rule

Element & At. NO.	Complex ion	e- lost in ion formation	e- gained by coordination	EAN	At. NO. of next inert gas
Fe – 26	$[Fe(CN)_6]^{4-}$	2	12	26-2 +12 = 36	36 Kr
Co – 27	$[Co(NH_3)_6]^{3+}$	3	12	27-3 +12 =36	36 Kr
Ni – 28	$[Ni(CO)_4]$	0	8	28-0 +8 =36	36 Kr
Pt – 78	$[Pt(NH_3)_6]^{4+}$	4	12	78 –4 +12= 86	86 Rn
Cu – 29	$[Fe(CN)_4]^{3-}$	1	8	29-1 +8 =36	36 Kr
Cr – 24	$[Cr(CO)_6]$	0	12	24-0 +12 =36	36 Kr

Table 4.2: Complexes not obeying EAN rule

Element & At. NO.	Complex ion	e- lost in ion formation	e- gained by coordination	EAN	At. NO. of next inert gas
Cr – 24	$[Cr(NH_3)_4]^{3+}$	3	12	24-3 +12 =33	36 Kr
Mn – 25	$[Mn(H_2O)_6]^{3+}$	3	12	25-3+12 = 34	36 Kr
Fe – 26	$[Fe(CN)_6]^{3-}$	3	12	26-3 +12 = 35	36 Kr
Co – 27	$[Co(NH_3)_5]^{3+}$	3	10	27-3+10 = 34	36 Kr
Ni – 28	$[Ni(NH_3)_6]^{2+}$	2	12	28-2 +12 =38	36 Kr
Pt – 78	$[Pt(NH_3)_4]^{2+}$	2	8	78–2 + 8 = 84	86 Rn

4.3 Definition of EAN

"The *total number of electrons associated with the central metal ion in a complex i.e. the number of electrons of metal ion plus electrons donated by the ligands, is called effective atomic number*." It may be either 36, 54 or 86. Sidgwick showed that for many metal ions, the effective atomic number is the same as the atomic number of next inert gas. In some cases (e.g. Cr^{3+}, Ni^{2+}, Fe^{3+}) however, it may be one or two units less or more.

These are exception of EAN rule, still they are stable. Hence as a theory, the EAN rule has little importance. However, as a rule of thumb, it is very useful in a limited group of coordination compounds. For any metal ion, EAN may be calculated by using the following formula.

$$EAN = (Z – n) + (2 \times C.N.)$$

Where, Z = atomic number of the metal.

N = number of electrons lost in cation formation.

C.N. = coordination number of the metal.

4.4 Limitations of Sidgwick model

i) The examples in the table show that EAN rule can't be uniformly applied to all complexes, there are many exceptions to EAN rule so that it cannot be considered as theory.

ii) Many complexes are quite stable even though they do not obey the EAN rule.

iii)   The ligands donate electron pairs and metal ion accepts them. Due to this it appears that there is an accumulation of negative charge on the metal ion. This decreases the stability of complex.

iv)   The $2s^2$ electron pair in NH_3 and H_2O, have no bonding characteristics.

v)   In many complexes such as fluoro or others the bonds between central metal ion and ligands are not covalent but predominantly ionic.

vi)   It gives no account of geometries of complexes.

Merits of EAN rule:

i)   It helps to understand the tendencies of the metals to coordinate with certain number of ligands. In other words, we can predict coordination number of the metal.

ii)   It explains stability of many coordination compounds.

4.5 Solved Problem on EAN

State following complexes obeys or not obeys EAN rule

1) $[Fe(CN)_6]^{3-}$

EAN = (Z – n) + (2 X C.N.)

$$= (26 - 3) + (2 \times 6)$$
$$= 23 + 12$$
$$= 35 \neq 36 \ (Kr)$$

Hence $[Fe(CN)_6]^{3-}$ does not obeys EAN rule

2) $[Pt(NH_3)_4]^{2+}$

EAN = (Z – n) + (2 X C.N.)

$$= (78 - 2) + (2 \times 4)$$
$$= 76 + 8$$
$$= 84 \neq 86 \ (Rn)$$

Hence $[Pt(NH_3)_4]^{2+}$ does not obeys EAN rule

3) $[Ni(CO)_4]$

EAN = (Z – n) + (2 X C.N.)

$$= (28 - 0) + (2 \times 4)$$
$$= 28 + 8$$
$$= 36 = 36 \ (Kr)$$

Hence $[Ni(CO)_4]$ obeys EAN rule

CHAPTER 5: VALENCE BOND THEORY OF COORDINATION COMPLEXES

5.1 Assumptions of Valence Bond Theory

1. For the formation of a coordinate covalent bond, the central atom or ion in the complex provides a number of empty orbitals equal to its coordination number. For this purpose, appropriate ligand orbitals are required.

2. For the formation of strong bond between the metal and the ligand, the overlap of metal orbitals with ligand orbitals should be as effective as possible. For this purpose, the original atomic orbitals of the metal may undergo hybridization to form a new set of equivalent orbitals with definite directional properties.

3. Each ligand must contain at least one pair of electrons for the purpose of donation and forming a σ bond.

4. A coordinate covalent sigma bond is formed when a vacant orbital of the metal overlap with the filled orbital of the ligand. The coordinate covalent bond thus has a considerable amount of polarity due to the mode of formation.

5. The metal electrons which do not take part in the hybridization occupy the inner d orbitals. They are known as non-bonding metal electrons.

6. There is also a possibility of formation of a π bond in addition to a σ bond. This is possible when filled d orbitals of the metal can overlap with

empty orbitals of the ligand. This kind of π bonding increases the strength of sigma bond and changes the charge distribution on both the metal and the ligand.

7. From the knowledge of the number of unpaired electrons in the complex thus formed, it is possible to predict the geometry and the magnetic properties of the complex and vice versa.

5.2 Concept of hybridization – Shapes and relative strengths of bonds

The combination of atomic orbitals to give mixed orbitals is known as hybridization. The combination of s and three p orbitals gives the tetrahedral hybrid sp^3 orbitals. Other hybrid orbitals are formed as the result of combination of s, p and d atomic orbitals. The shape of some hybrid orbitals are shown below in table 5.1.

Table 5.1: Shape of some Molecular Orbitals and relative bond Strength

Sr. No.	Hybrid Orbitals	Type of molecule	Molecular shape	Relative bond strength	Example of complexes
1)	sp	Linear		1.93	$[Ag(NH_3)_2]^+$ $[Ag(CN)_2]^-$
2)	Sp^2	Trigonal planar		1.99	$[Ag(R_3P)_3]^+$
3)	Sp^3 or sd^3 (dxy,dyz, dxz)	Tetrahedral		2.0	$[Ni(CO)_4]$ $[Zn(NH_3)_4]^{2+}$
4)	dsp^2 (dx^2-y^2)	Square planar		2.69	$[Ni(CN)_4]^{2-}$ $[Pt(NH_3)_4]^{2+}$
5)	dsp^3 or sp^3d (dz^2)	Trigonal bipyramidal			$[Cu(Cl_5)]^{3-}$ $[Fe(CO)_5]$

Sr. No.	Hybrid Orbitals	Type of molecule	Molecular shape	Relative bond strength	Example of complexes
6)	dsp^3 or sp^3d (dx^2-y^2)	Square pyramidal	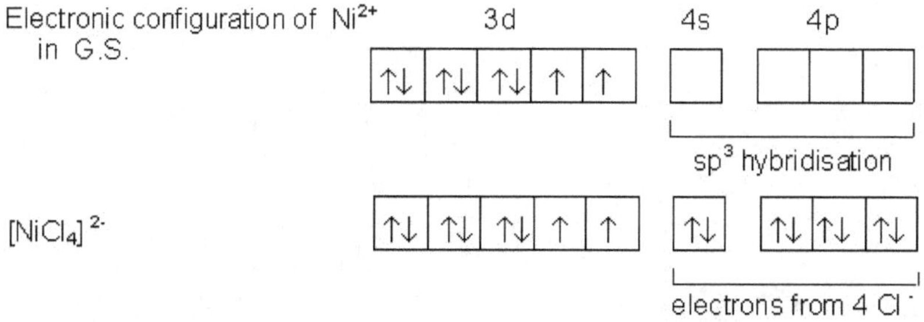		$[Ni(PEt_3)_2Br_3]$ $[SbF_5]^{2-}$
7)	d^2sp^3 or sp^3d^2 (dx^2-y^2)(dz^2)	Octahedral		2.92	$[Co(NH_3)_6]^{3+}$ $[Fe(CN)_6]^{3-}$

5.3 Bonding in Coordinate Complexes

5.3.1 Tetrahedral complexes formed by sp^3 hybridization.

Example 1- $[NiCl_4]^{2-}$

Electronic configuration of $_{28}Ni$ – $1s^2, 2s^2, 2p^6, 3s^2, 3p^6, 4s^2, 3d^8$

Electronic configuration of Ni^{2+} – $1s^2, 2s^2, 2p^6, 3s^2, 3p^6, 4s^0, 3d^8$

The observed magnetic moment of the complex is 2.95 BM. The calculated magnetic moment of the complex is 2.82 BM. The two values are close. This shows that the complex ion has two unpaired electrons and it is paramagnetic. The sp^3 hybridization suggests tetrahedral geometry. In practice, the observed geometry of the complex is tetrahedral.

Example 2- $[MnCl_4]^{2-}$

Electronic configuration of $_{25}Mn$ – $1s^2, 2s^2, 2p^6, 3s^2, 3p^6, 4s^2, 3d^5$

Electronic configuration of Mn^{2+} – $1s^2, 2s^2, 2p^6, 3s^2, 3p^6, 4s^0, 3d^5$

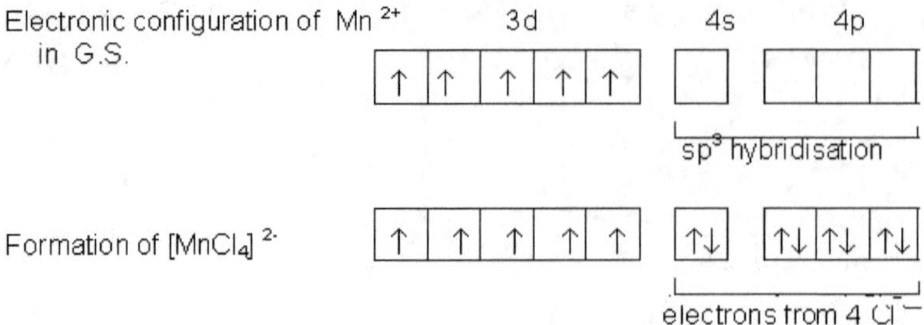

The observed magnetic moment of the complex is 5.95 BM. The calculated magnetic moment of the complex is 5.92 BM. The two values are close. This shows that the complex ion has five unpaired electrons and it is paramagnetic. The sp^3 hybridization suggests tetrahedral geometry. In practice, the observed geometry of the complex is tetrahedral.

5.3.2 Square Planar Complexes formed by dsp² hybridization

Example 1- [Ni (CN)₄]²⁻

Electronic configuration of $_{28}Ni$ – $1s^2, 2s^2, 2p^6, 3s^2, 3p^6, 4s^2, 3d^8$

Electronic configuration of Ni^{2+} – $1s^2, 2s^2, 2p^6, 3s^2, 3p^6, 4s^0, 3d^8$

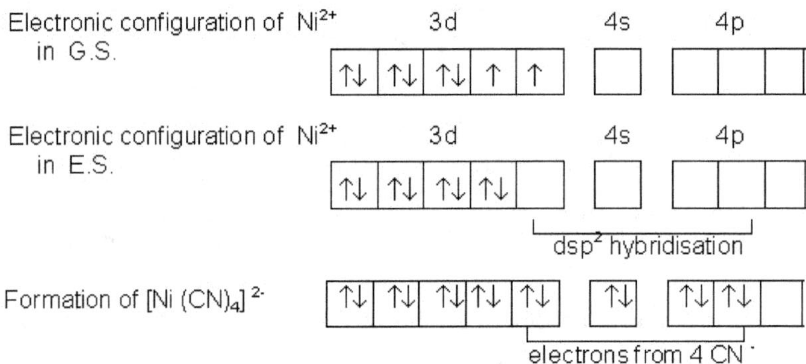

The unpaired electrons in the ground state of Ni^{2+} ion, pair up in the excited state. The pairing energy is supplied by the formation of four strong bonds in the complex. Since all the electrons are paired, the $[Ni (CN)_4]^{2-}$ complex ion becomes diamagnetic. The observed & calculated magnetic moment of the complex is zero. The central metal ion undergoes dsp^2 hybridization and the complex ion takes square planar geometry.

Example 2-   [Cu (NH$_3$)$_4$]$^{2+}$

Electronic configuration of $_{29}$Cu – 1s^2, 2s^2, 2p^6, 3s^2, 3p^6, 4s^2, 3d^9

Electronic configuration of Cu^{2+} – 1s^2, 2s^2, 2p^6, 3s^2, 3p^6, 4s^0, 3d^9

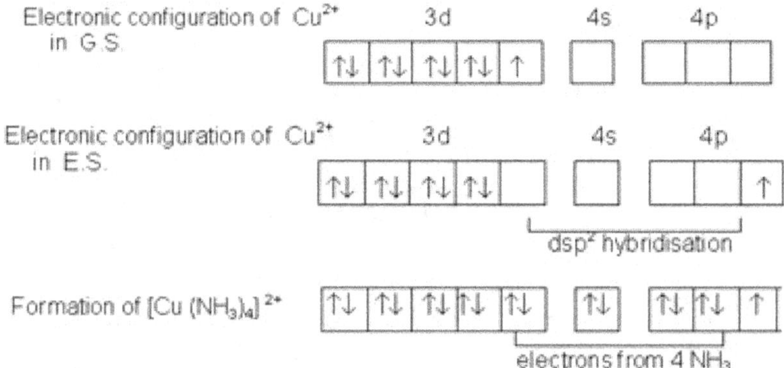

This complex ion has a square planar geometry. It is paramagnetic and has magnetic moment 1.8 BM. This shows that the complex ion has one unpaired electron and it is paramagnetic. The central metal ion undergoes dsp^2 hybridization and the complex ion takes square planar geometry.

The promotion of one electron from 3d to 4p orbital is not completely satisfactory. The 4p electron would be expected to be easily lost which means that the complex could be easily oxidized from Cu^{2+} to Cu^{3+}. But this is not so.

If we place the unpaired electron in the 3d orbital, it would suggest sp^3 hybridization. That would suggest a tetrahedral geometry which is contrary to the observation.The use of 4d orbital (outer orbital) to form sp^{2}d hybridization is also not possible because the promotion energy would be too high and that would make the complex unstable. However, the complex is highly stable.

The failure to explain satisfactory explanation of the bonding in stable complexes such as [Cu (NH$_3$)$_4$] $^{2+}$ is a major weakness of the VBT.

Octahedral Complexes are formed by d^{2}sp^3 or sp^{3}d^2 hybridization

5.3.3 Octahedral Complexes formed by d^{2}sp^3 hybridization

1) d^{2}sp^3 hybridization: When two orbitals, (d$_{x^2-y^2}$) and d$_{z^2}$ of (n-1) shell, one s-orbital of last shell n, take part in hybridization, it is known as d^{2}sp^3 hybridization.

Example 1- [Co (NH₃)₆]³⁺

Electronic configuration of $_{27}$Co – $1s^2, 2s^2, 2p^6, 3s^2, 3p^6, 4s^2, 3d^7$

Electronic configuration of Co³⁺ – $1s^2, 2s^2, 2p^6, 3s^2, 3p^6, 4s^0, 3d^6$

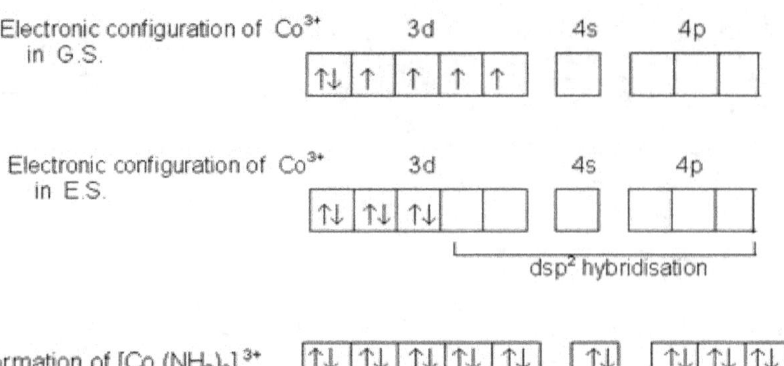

The four unpaired electrons in the ground state of Co³⁺ ion, pair up in the excited state. Thus, two vacant d orbitals are created. Since all the electrons are paired, the [Co (NH₃)₆]³⁺ ion becomes diamagnetic. The observed & calculated magnetic moment of the complex is zero. The pairing energy is supplied by the formation of six strong bonds in the complex. The central metal ion undergoes d $^2sp^3$ hybridization and the complex ion takes octahedral geometry.

Example 2 - [Fe(CN)₆]³⁻

Electronic configuration of $_{26}$Fe – $1s^2, 2s^2, 2p^6, 3s^2, 3p^6, 4s^2, 3d^6$

Electronic configuration of Fe³⁺ – $1s^2, 2s^2, 2p^6, 3s^2, 3p^6, 4s^0, 3d^5$

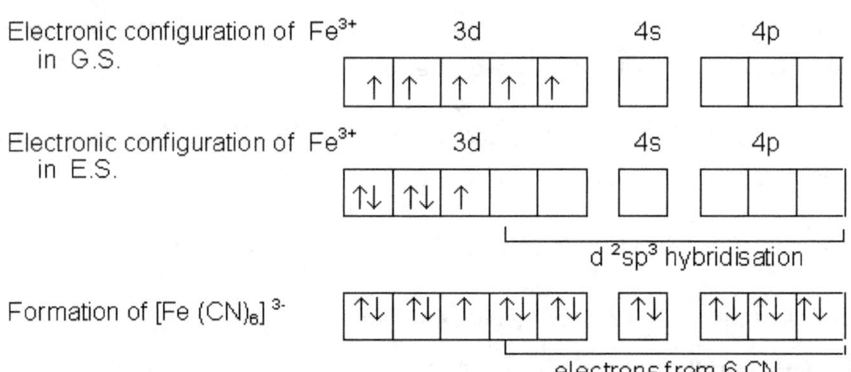

The five unpaired electrons in the ground state of Fe³⁺ ion, pair up in the excited state. Thus, two vacant d orbitals are created. This leaves one unpaired electron in one d orbital. The [Fe (CN)$_6$]$^{3-}$ ion becomes paramagnetic. The observed magnetic moment of the complex is 2.3 BM & calculated magnetic moment of the complex is 1.73 BM. The central metal ion undergoes d^{2}sp^3 hybridization and the complex ion takes octahedral geometry.

5.3.4 Octahedral Complexes formed by sp^{3}d^2 hybridization

When one s orbital, three p orbital and two d orbitals (d$_{x^2-y^2}$) and d$_{z^2}$ of the same shell i.e. the last shell take part in hybridization, it is known as sp^{3}d^2 hybridization. The explanation of bonding for some octahedral complexes can be given in a similar way but central metal ion in these complexes undergoes sp^{3}d^2 hybridization instead of d ^{2}sp^3 hybridization and keeps the same number of unpaired electron as in the free ion. The sp^{3}d^{2}complex have the same geometry as that of d^{2}sp^3 complex.

Example 1- [FeF$_6$]$^{3-}$

Electronic configuration of $_{26}$Fe – 1s^2, 2s^2, 2p^6, 3s^2, 3p^6, 4s^2, 3d^6

Electronic configuration of Fe^{3+} – 1s^2, 2s^2, 2p^6, 3s^2, 3p^6, 4s^0, 3d^5

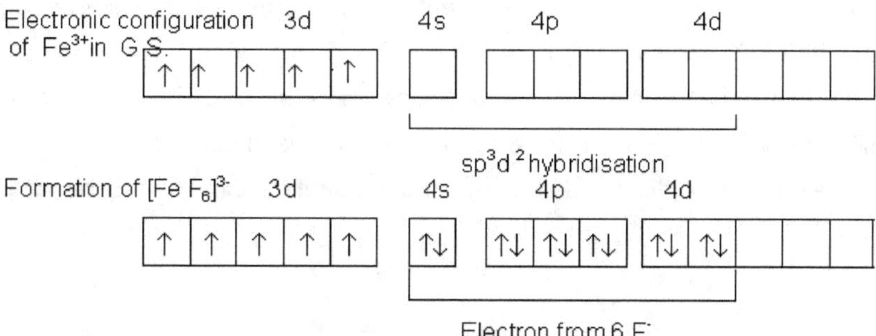

There are five unpaired electrons in the free Fe^{3+} ion so also five unpaired electrons in the [Fe F$_6$]$^{3-}$ complex ion. The complex ion is found to be paramagnetic. The observed magnetic moment suggests the presence of five unpaired electrons. The complex ion is octahedral in shape.

Example 1- [Ni(NH$_3$)$_6$]$^{2+}$

Electronic configuration of $_{28}$Ni – 1s^2, 2s^2, 2p^6, 3s^2, 3p^6, 4s^2, 3d^8

Electronic configuration of Ni^{2+} – 1s^2, 2s^2, 2p^6, 3s^2, 3p^6, 4s^0, 3d^8

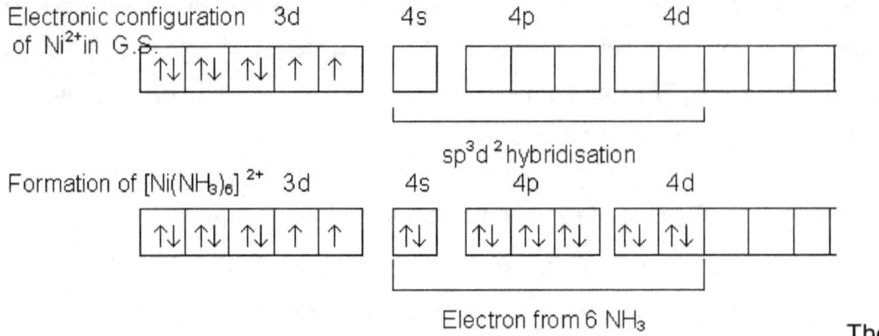

There are two unpaired electrons in the free Ni^{2+} ion so also two unpaired electrons in the $[Ni(NH_3)_6]^{2+}$ complex ion. The complex ion is found to be paramagnetic. The observed magnetic moment suggests the presence of two unpaired electrons. The complex ion is octahedral in shape.

5.4 Inner and outer orbital complexes

Paling's theory faces difficulties when the number of orbitals needed to accommodate the bonding electrons is too low. This can result from the occupancy of the orbitals by either paired or unpaired electrons from the metal ion. e.g. $[Fe\,F_6]^{3-}$ and $[Ni(NH_3)_6]^{2+}$ which have magnetic moment corresponding to five and two unpaired electrons respectively. In either of these cases, it is not possible to have d^2sp^3 hybridization of the central metal ion is as shown below, there are only four orbitals (4s and 4p) of approximately same energy beyond the occupied orbital.

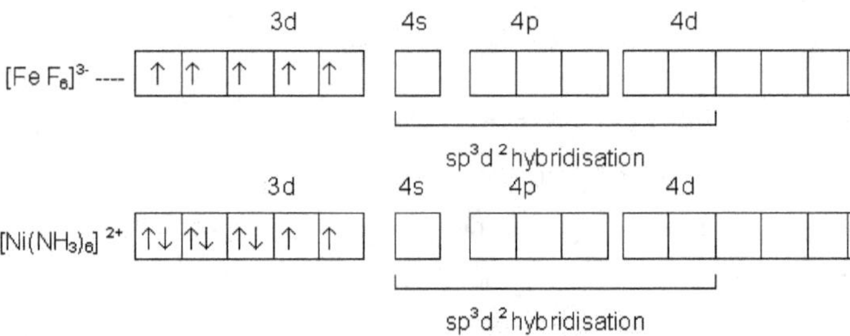

Huggins, in 1937, proposed that outer d orbital might be used in bond formation. However, at that time, it was generally considered that the 4d orbitals could not hybridize satisfactorily with 4s and 4p orbitals to give strong covalent octahedral bonds. Craig showed that with highly electronegative ligands the use of 4d orbitals probably leads to stronger bonds than those formed by 4s & 4p orbitals alone.

In general, inner orbital octahedral complexes utilize $(n-1)d^2$, ns, np^3 orbitals and show d^2sp^3 hybridization and outer orbital octahedral complexes utilize ns, np^3, nd^2 orbitals and show sp^3d^2 hybridization, where n is the principal number of the outermost shell. The octahedral complexes like $[Co(NH_3)_6]^{3+}$ which utilize (n-1)d, ns & np orbitals of the metal ion to show d^2sp^3 hybridization are called **inner orbital complexes**.

Whereas the octahedral complexes like $[Ni(NH_3)_6]^{2+}$ which utilize ns, np & nd orbitals of the metal ion to show sp^3d^2 hybridization **outer orbital complexes**. Inner orbital complexes are also called low spin or spin paired because in contain more number of unpaired electrons, while outer orbital complexes are called spin free or high spin.

5.5 Electroneutrality principle

One of the objections raised to Pauling VBT of coordination compound was that there would be an accumulation of negative charge on the central metal atom or ion during the formation of a complex. The charge developed on the metal and the ligand due to the shift of the electron pair is called as formal charge. Thus in octahedral complexes, the formal charge on Fe in $[Fe(H_2O)_6]^{3+}$ is -3, in $[Fe(H_2O)_6]^{2+}$ is -4, in $[Fe(CN)_6]^{4-}$ is -4. The formal charge on the central metal is obtained by subtracting the original charge on the metal from the total number of electron pairs shared between the metal and the ligands. for e.g. $[Fe(H_2O)_6]^{2+}$, the original charge on Fe is +2 while the charge due to the six electron pairs shared between Fe and H2O is -6. Thus, the formal charge on the Fe would be (-6 + 2) = - 4 Pauling suggested that such a situation would not arise, due to two reasons -

1) Generally, ligands are fairly electronegative hence the electrons will not be shared equally between the metal and the ligands thus inducing positive charge on the metal to balance the unfavorable formal charge and

2) The complex would be most stable when electronegativity of the ligand was such that the metal achieved essentially a neutral condition. This rule is known as electroneutrality principle.

Pauling electroneutrality principle states that ***"electrons are distributed in a molecule in such a way as to make the residual charge on each atom zero or very nearly zero except that hydrogen and the most electronegative metals can acquire partial positive charge and the most electronegative atoms can acquire partial negative charge".*** The charge on the atom is decreased by (i) a change in the polarity or (ii) a change in the amount of ionic character of a bond.

This principle is applicable to complexes which are unstable because of the accumulation of the excessive negative charge on the metal. In such complexes bonds are partially ionic and partially covalent. We can illustrate the principle by taking an example of the complex ion $Fe(H_2O)_6]^{3+}$. If all the Fe - O bonds are 100% ionic, then entire charge 3+ would be located on the Fe atom.

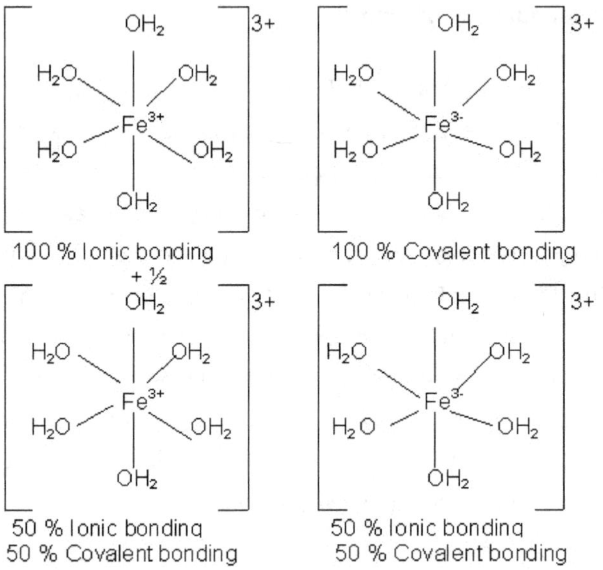

100 % Ionic bonding

100 % Covalent bonding

50 % Ionic bonding
50 % Covalent bonding

50 % Ionic bonding
50 % Covalent bonding

This implies that electrons are not shared and the electrons are not shared and the electrons of the ligands remain with oxygen atoms only. If all the Fe-O bonds are 100% covalent i.e. there is equal sharing of electrons between Fe and O atoms of ligands, the formal charge on Fe would be (-6 +3) = -3. When oxygen atom donates an electron pair it gets +1 formal charge and Fe atom gets –1 formal charge. Thus in 100% covalent bonding, each oxygen gets +1 formal charge and Fe would be left with (-6 +3) = -3 formal charge.

If the Fe – O bonds are 50% ionic and 50% covalent each oxygen would get + ½ formal charge and Fe would get – ½ formal charge per shared pair of electrons. Since Fe shares six electron pairs, it would get 6 x (- ½) = -3 charge which would be cancelled by its original charge +3. Thus, the residual charge on Fe would be zero. However oxygen atom would be reluctant to bear a positive charge and therefore electrons of hydrogen atoms would be displaced towards oxygen atom. The net effect would be that each hydrogen atom would get + ¼ formal charge. Thus, the oxygen atoms become neutral. The +3 charge, which was distributed on oxygen atoms, would now share by 12 hydrogen atoms when the bonds are 50% ionic. Thus the shift of electron pairs and charge distribution takes place in such a way that the formal charge –3 on Fe is neutralized. This gives stability of the complex. This is shown below.

5.6 Multiple bonding

According to VBT **ligand must contain at least one lone pair of electrons for the purpose of donation and forming a σ bond**. There are many ligands such as CO, RNC, PX_3 (X- halogens), PR_3, AsR_3, SR_2 etc. which are very poor electron donors and yet they forms many stable metallic complexes.

Pauling supposed that atoms of transition metals are capable of forming multiple bonds with electron accepting groups by making use of the electrons and orbitals of the shell below the valence shell. That is, in addition to sigma bond, a π bond may be formed between the metal and ligand. In this case, electrons are donated by the metal to the ligand to form the π bond. This back bonding in which the metal shares its own pair of electrons with the ligand, offset the accumulation of negative charge on the metal and strengthens the σ bond.

There are mainly two types of π bonding found in the complexes.
1)   Donation of electrons from metal d orbitals (t_2g) to empty p orbitals of the ligands. This type of bonding is generally referred to as **dπ-pπ**

bonding. It occurs when the ligand contains an atom from second row e.g. N in NO_2^-, C in CO, or C in CN^-.

2) Donation of electrons from metal d orbitals (t_2g) to empty d orbitals of the ligands. This type of bonding is generally referred to as **dπ-dπ bonding**. It occurs when the ligand contains an atom from third or later row e.g. P, S etc.

Ni-C bond distance in $Ni(CO)_4$ is shorter than that expected for a single bond. This suggests that the bond has an appreciable amount of double bond character. The VB representation of the metal –carbon double bond requires that the carbon –oxygen bond be changed to double bond in order to vacate a p orbital for dπ-pπ bonding.

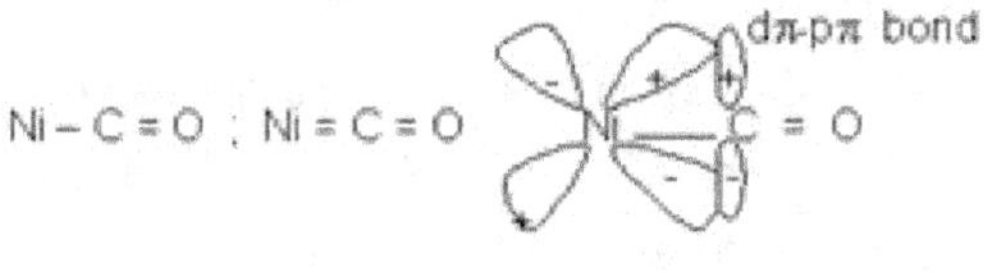

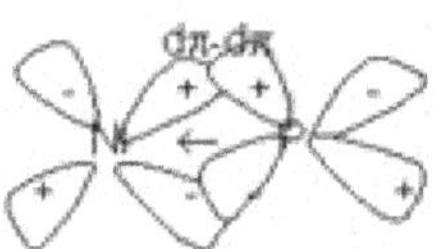

Figure 5.1: Metal - Ligand dπ-pπ bonding

Figure 5.2: Metal - Ligand dπ-dπ bonding

Let us consider a bonding between a metal like Ni, which has an available nonbonding pair of d electrons, and a ligand like PX_3, which is a poor Lewis base. The filled d orbital on the metal overlaps with one of the empty d orbitals of phosphorus giving to dπ-dπ bonding.

5.7 Limitations of Valence Bond Theory

Pauling VBT when applied to complexes has following drawbacks.

1. It gives only qualitative explanation regarding the structure, bonding and magnetic properties of complexes. It fails to give any quantitative explanation of these properties.
2. It can't explain or interpret the spectra of the complexes.
3. It can't explain why certain complexes are more liable than others.

4.   It can' account for or predict detailed magnetic properties.

5.   In VBT it is assumed that all d orbitals are of equal energy. It does not consider the splitting of the d energy levels.

6.   It does not account for the relative energies of different structures.

7.   It fails to account for the observed geometries of certain complexes e.g. the tetragonal and distorted octahedral complexes.

8.   It does not tell us why water and halide ions commonly form high spin complexes while cyanide ions form low spin complexes.   e.g. why $[NiCl_4]^{2-}$ is a high spin complex with a square planar geometry.

9.   It does not give us any satisfactory reason for the formation of inner and outer orbital complexes.

In spite of these limitations, it can be said that VBT is simple and easy to apply and makes a good beginning to explain many things about the complexes.

CHAPTER 6: CRYSTAL FIELD THEORY OF COORDINATION COMPLEXES

6.1 Introduction

Hybridization suggested by Pauling helped to interpret the geometrical shape of complexes but hybridization by itself, failed to account for the voluminous data which rapidly accumulated.

There were unexplained differences between measured and calculated magnetic moments. Compound were found which had intermediate values for their magnetic moments, the distinction between ionic and covalent bonding in complexes seemed to be confusing. Difficulties arise for interpretation of geometrical shapes e.g. the square planar shape of $[Cu(NH_3)_4]^{2+}$ and particularly distorted shapes.

To overcome this difficulty, Bethe and Van Vleck introduced a new theory and it is mainly applied for ionic crystals this theory is named as crystal field theory. Orgel had developed the general aspects of this theory. On the basis of this theory, a complex is regarded as an aggregation of central ion surrounded by other ions or molecules with electrical dipoles. The electrical dipole of central ion will affect the surrounding ligands while the combined field of the ligands is particularly marked on the d electrons, which play such a large part in complex formation, by transition elements. The influence of the ligands depends on their geometrical positions in the complex.

In the simple bonding between the central ion and ligands are purely ionic so that the forces involved can be limited to electrostatic forces. This theory does not consider covalent bonding. Such a limited treatment is generally referred as CFT. The modified treatment which includes covalent bonding is called Ligand field Theory.

6.2 Shapes of 'd' orbitals

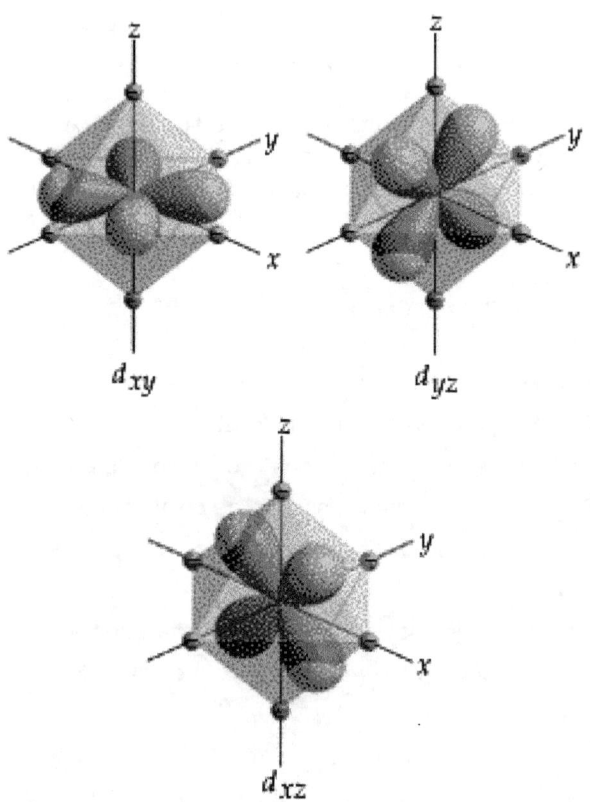

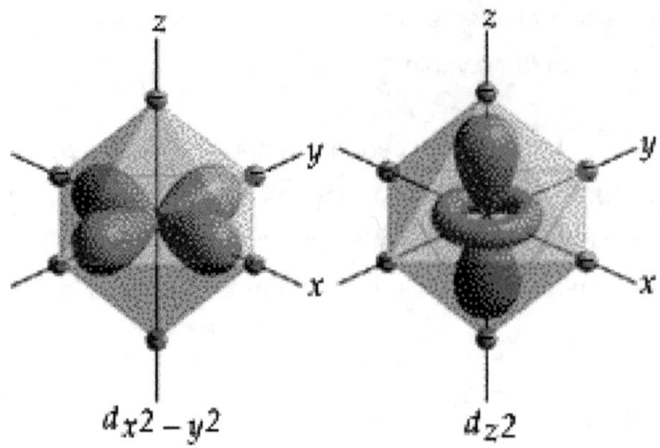

Figure 6.1: Shape five d orbitals

All the five d orbitals are not identical and there are in fact two sets. **The $d_x{}^2{}_{-y}{}^2$ and $d_z{}^2$ orbitals form one set** and have lobes lying along the mutually perpendicular x, y and z axes. The **d_{xy}, d_{yz} and d_{xz} orbitals form second set** and have lobes pointing between the axes. The shape of d orbitals is shown in figure 6.1.

6.3 Assumptions of Crystal field theory

i)   In a complex, the transition metal ion is placed in the center and it is surrounded by ligands with lone pairs of electrons.

ii)   The ligands are either negative ions like CN^- or Cl^- or they are molecules like H_2O, NH_3 and they are considered as point charges. If the ligands is a neutral molecule, then the negative end of the dipole is directed towards the metal ion.

iii)   There is no interaction between the metal orbitals and ligand orbitals.

iv)   The attraction between the metal ion and the ligand is purely electrostatic i.e. the bond is 100% ionic.

v)   The electrons of the metal ion are repelled by the negative field of the ligands and therefore the metal electrons occupy those d orbital which have their lobes farthest away from the direction of the ligands.

vi)   The number of ligands and their arrangement around the metal ion determine the nature and strength of the crystal field.

vii)   The degeneracy of d orbitals of the free metal ion is removed by the ligands when a complex is formed.

6.4 Group Theoretical symbols

$d_{x^2-y^2}$ and d_{z^2} orbitals are collectively denoted as e_g and the d_{xy}, d_{yz} and d_{xz} orbitals are collectively denoted as t_{2g}. The symbol t means there are three degenerate orbitals (d_{xy}, d_{yz} and d_{xz}) (that are equal in energy   i.e. they are degenerate). The symbol g stands for gerade (German – even). The orbital is said to gerade if it is centrosymmetric. i.e. it has the same sign of the wave function at the same distance in opposite direction from the center of symmetry. The symbol u stands for ungerade (German- uneven). The orbital is said to ungerade if it changes the sign of the wave function at the same distance in opposite direction from the center of symmetry. The s and d orbitals are 'g' i.e. gerade and p and f orbitals are 'u' i.e. ungerade. The e_g orbitals are doubly degenerate while t_{2g} orbitals are triply degenerate.

In addition to these symbols, sometimes the subscript 1 and 2 are also used. The subscript 1 and 2 means respectively that the orbital or orbitals do not change sign on rotation about the Cartesian axes and that they do not change sign on rotation about axes diagonal to the Cartesian axes. Thus, the metal s and p orbitals are designated a_{1g} and t_{1u}. The symbol a denotes a singly degenerate orbital.

6.5 Splitting of d orbitals

In a free ion, the five d orbitals are degenerate (i.e. energically equal) and electrons which occupy such orbitals do so according to the rule of maximum multiplicity. CFT is basically concerned with the effect of different arrangements of surrounding ligands on the energy of the d orbitals. The ligands exert an electrostatic field which tends to repel the electrons, particularly the outer d orbitals, of the central metal ion. This repulsion raises the energy levels of the d orbital in the central metal ion. If the d orbitals were all alike and the ligand field affected them all in the same way, the five d orbitals would remain degenerate at a higher energy level. This is shown in figure 6.2.

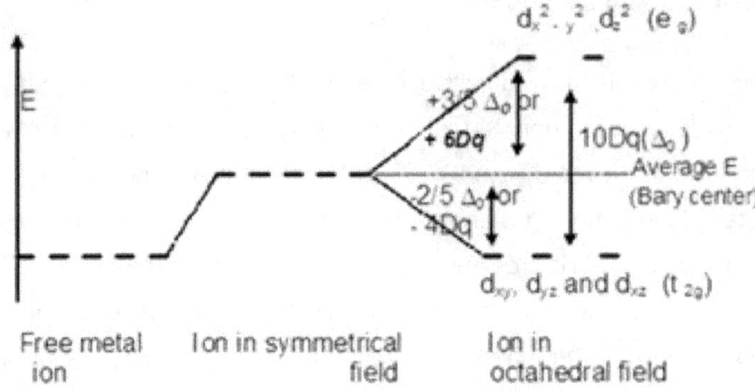

Figure 6.2 Crystal field splitting in an octahedral field

In fact, the d orbitals are not all alike. They form two groups according to their orientation in space. Those d orbitals lying in the direction of the ligands are repelled more and raised in energy with respect to those lying away from the ligands.

As a result, the degeneracy of the d orbitals of the metal ion is split by the ligand field or the energies of the d orbitals becomes differentiated in presence of the ligands. This effect is known as crystal field splitting. Splitting of d orbitals are shown in figure 6.2. This concept forms the basis of crystal field theory. By preferentially filling the low-lying d orbitals by electrons, the complex may be stabilized. The gain in bonding energy achieved in this way is called Crystal Field stabilization Energy (C.F.S.E.).

6.6 Application of C.F.T. to Octahedral Complexes

In an octahedral complex, it assumed, that the metal is at the center of the octahedron and the ligands are at the six corners of the octahedron. This is shown in figure 6.3. The e_g orbitals ($d_{x^2-y^2}$ and d_{z^2} orbitals) are directed along the axes and the t_{2g} orbitals (d_{xy}, d_{yz} and d_{xz} orbitals) point in between the axes x, y and z. It follows that approach of six ligands along the x, y, z, -x, -y and –z directions will increase the energy of the $d_{x^2-y^2}$ and d_{z^2} orbitals which point along the axes much more than d_{xy}, d_{yz} and d_{xz} orbitals which point in between the axes. Thus under the influence of an octahedral ligand field the d orbital split into two groups of different energies. This is shown in figure 6.2.

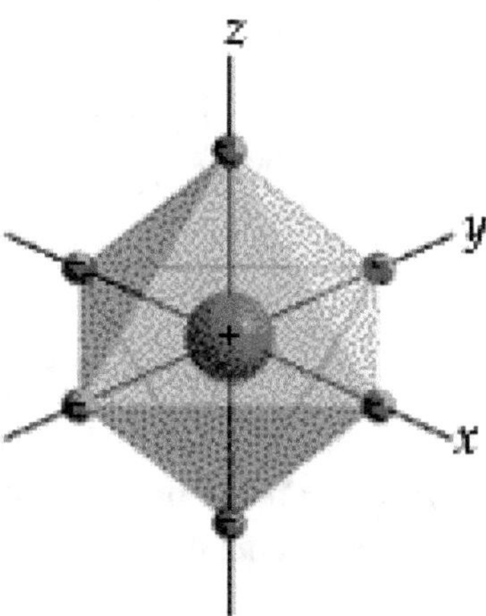

Figure 6.3: The octahedral arrangement of six ligands around a central ion. The ligands lie on the x, y and z axes.

The average energy is called the **bary center**. The difference in energy between the two sets t_{2g} and e_g is given either of the symbol $10D_q$ or (Δ_0). It is measured in terms of a parameter called D_q. This quantity may be small or large but is always taken arbitrarily as $10\ D_q$. It follows that the e_g orbitals are $+3/5\ \Delta_0$ or $(+6D_q)$ above the average level and the t_{2g} orbitals are $-2/5\ \Delta_0$ or $-\ 4D_q$ below the average level.

6.7 Strong and weak Ligand Field Splitting

In an octahedral complex, if the value of **$10D_q$ or (Δ_0) is large**, it is called a **strong field splitting** and the complex is referred to as a **strong field complex**. If the value of **$10D_q$ or (Δ_0) is small**, it is called a **weak field splitting** and the complex is referred to as a **weak field complex**. Figure 6.4 shows strong field and weak field splitting in an octahedral complex.

The magnitude of $10D_q$ or (Δ_0) depends upon three factors-

i)   The nature of the ligand

ii)   The charge on the metal ion.

iii)   Whether the metal is in first, second and third row of transition elements.

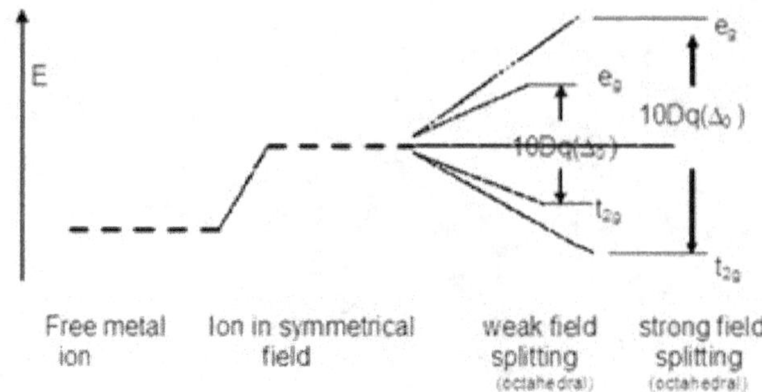

Figure 6.4 Crystal field splitting of metal d orbitals in weak and strong octahedral ligand field

Ligands, which cause only a **small degree of splitting**, are termed as **weak ligands** and those, which cause a **large splitting**, are called **strong ligands**. The common ligands can be arranged in order of their strength and this series is called the **spectrochemical series**. It is given below.

$$CN^- > NO_2^- > \text{------} > H_2O \approx C_2O_4 > OH^- > F^- > Cl^- > I^-$$

Thus CN^- produces almost double the splitting than the Cl^- ion.

6.8 Distribution of electrons in d orbitals

The d orbitals are filled in by electrons according to following rules.

i) The electron will occupy the orbital of lowest energy first.

ii) Hund's rule of maximum multiplicity will be followed i.e. electrons with not pair up unless all degenerate orbitals contain one electron each i.e. they are half filled.

iii) If the energy required to occupy the higher energy orbital (say e_g) is greater than the energy required to pair up the electron (called pairing energy P) in the lower energy orbital (say t_{2g}) i.e. if $10D_q$ or $\Delta_0 > P$, the electron will pair up in the lower energy orbital.

iv) If the energy required to occupy the higher energy orbital (say e_g) is less than the energy required to pair up the electron (called pairing energy P) in the lower energy orbital (say t_{2g}) i.e. if $10D_q$ or $\Delta_0 < P$, the electron will occupy the higher energy orbital.

Let us consider the filling of t_{2g} and e_g orbitals in an octahedral complex. The d^1, d^2 and d^3 electrons will occupy the t_{2g} orbitals following Hund's rule. This filling will be the same in the strong field and weak field complex. However, for a d^4 system, occupancy of the t_{2g} and e_g orbitals will be different in a strong field and weak field complex. Figure 6.5 shows distribution of d^4 electron in the strong field and weak field complex. In the strong field complex $\Delta_0 > P$, so the fourth electron pairs up in the t_{2g} orbital and gives the electron configuration of the metal as t_{2g}^4, e_g^0. In the weak field complex $\Delta_0 < P$, so the fourth electron occupies e_g orbital and gives the electron configuration of the metal as t_{2g}^3, e_g^1.

Table 6.1: Distribution of d electron in t_{2g} and e_g sets in strong octahedral ligand field

(n= no. of unpaired electrons, S= resultant spin)

$d^{n\ ion}$	Distribution of d electrons in		n	S = n/2
	t_{2g} set	e_g set		
d^1	↑		1	0.5
d^2	↑ ↑		2	1.0
d^3	↑ ↑ ↑		3	1.5
d^4	↑↓ ↑ ↑		2	1.0
d^5	↑↓ ↑↓ ↑		1	0.5
d^6	↑↓ ↑↓ ↑↓		0	0.0
d^7	↑↓ ↑↓ ↑↓	↑	1	0.5
d^8	↑↓ ↑↓ ↑↓	↑ ↑	2	1.0
d^9	↑↓ ↑↓ ↑↓	↑↓ ↑	1	0.5
d^{10}	↑↓ ↑↓ ↑↓	↑↓ ↑↓	0	0.0

Similar argument can be made about the occupancy of t_{2g} and e_g orbitals for d^5 to d^{10} system of electrons strong field and weak field complex. The complexes formed by strong ligands (strong field complexes) have the minimum number of unpaired electrons, so the complexes are called **low spin** or **spin paired** complexes. The complexes formed by weak ligands (weak field complexes) have the maximum number of unpaired electrons, so such complexes are called **high spin** or **spin free** complexes.

Table 6.1 & 6.2 shows distribution of d electrons in a strong field and weak field octahedral complex respectively.

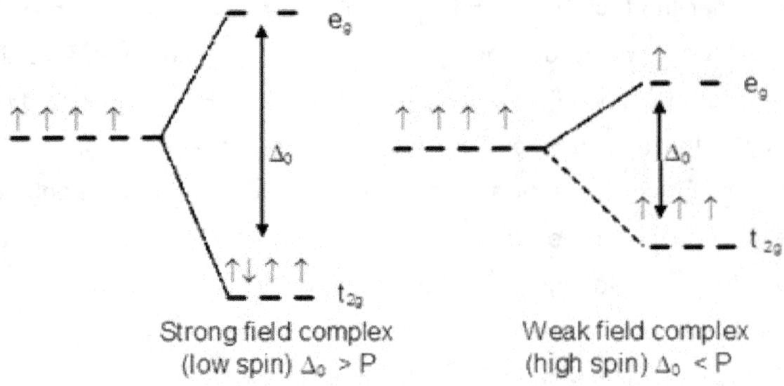

Figure 6.5: d^4 system in strong and weak field

Table 6.2: Distribution of d electron in t_{2g} and e_g sets in weak octahedral ligand field

(n= no. of unpaired electrons, S= resultant spin)

$d^{n \text{ ion}}$	Distribution of d electrons in		n	S = n/2
	t_{2g} set	e_g set		
d^1	↑		1	0.5
d^2	↑ ↑		2	1.0
d^3	↑ ↑ ↑		3	1.5
d^4	↑ ↑ ↑	↑	4	2.0
d^5	↑ ↑ ↑	↑ ↑	5	2.5
d^6	↑↓ ↑ ↑	↑ ↑	4	2.0
d^7	↑↓ ↑↓ ↑	↑ ↑	3	1.5
d^8	↑↓ ↑↓ ↑↓	↑ ↑	2	1.0
d^9	↑↓ ↑↓ ↑↓	↑↓ ↑	1	0.5
d^{10}	↑↓ ↑↓ ↑↓	↑↓ ↑↓	0	0.0

6.9 Crystal Field stabilization Energy (C.F.S.E.) of Octahedral Complexes

The total decrease in energy caused by the splitting of the d orbitals and their occupancy by electrons is called Crystal Field stabilization Energy (C.F.S.E.). In case there is pairing energy involved it is added to the CFSE. The CFSE is given by the formula.

CFSE (Octahedral) = [-4D$_q$ x No. of e$^-$ in t$_{2g}$ orbitals] + [+6D$_q$ x No. of e$^-$ in e$_g$ orbitals]

1. for d^1 system (t$_{2g}$)^1 CFSE = [-4Dq x 1]   = -4Dq
2. for d^2 system (t$_{2g}$)^2 CFSE = [-4Dq x 2]   = -8Dq
3. for d^3 system (t$_{2g}$)^3 CFSE = [-4Dq x 3]   = -12Dq
4. for d^8 system (t$_{2g}$)^6 (e$_g$)^2 CFSE = [-4Dq x 6] + [+6Dq x 2] +3P   = -12Dq + 3P
5. for d^9 system (t$_{2g}$)^6 (e$_g$)^3 CFSE = [-4Dq x 6] + [+6Dq x 3] +3P   = -6Dq + 4P
6. for d^{10} system (t$_{2g}$)^6 (e$_g$)^4 CFSE = [-4Dq x 6] + [+6Dq x 4]   = 0

They will be the same for strong and weak field complexes. For d^{10} system, although five electrons get paired they create a spherical crystal field around the metal ion and the net CFSE is zero. The **CFSE for d^4, d^5, d^6 and d^8 system in strong field and weak field octahedral complexes are different.** They can be calculated as follows.

In a strong field complex

1. for d^4 system (t$_{2g}$)^4 CFSE = [-4Dq x 4] + P = -16Dq + P

2. for d^5 system (t$_{2g}$)^5 CFSE = [-4Dq x 5] + 2P = -20Dq + 2P
3. for d^6 system (t$_{2g}$)^6 CFSE = [-4Dq x 6] + 3P = -24Dq + 3P
4. for d^7 system (t$_{2g}$)^6 (e$_g$)^1 CFSE = [-4Dq x 6] + [+6Dq x 1] +3P = -18Dq + 3P

For a weak field complex

1. for d^4 system (t$_{2g}$)^3 (e$_g$)^1 CFSE = [-4Dq x 3] + [+6Dq x 1] = -6Dq
2. for d^5 system (t$_{2g}$)^3 (e$_g$)^2 CFSE = [-4Dq x 3] + [+6Dq x 2] = 0
3. for d^6 system (t$_{2g}$)^4 (e$_g$)^2 CFSE = [-4Dq x 4] + [+6Dq x 2] + P = -4Dq + P
4. for d^7 system (t$_{2g}$)^5 (e$_g$)^2 CFSE = [-4Dq x 5] + [+6Dq x 2] +2P = -8Dq + 2P

Table 6.3 shows the CFSE values from d^1 to d^{10} system for strong field and weak field octahedral complexes.

Table 6.3: CFSE in Weak & Strong Field Ligands

d^n	Weak field configuration	Unpaired electron	CFSE	Strong field configuration	Unpaired electron	CFSE
d^1	t_{2g}^1	1	-4Dq	t_{2g}^1	1	-4Dq
d^2	t_{2g}^2	2	-8Dq	t_{2g}^2	2	-8Dq
d^3	t_{2g}^3	3	-12Dq	t_{2g}^3	3	-12Dq
d^4	$t_{2g}^3\ e_g^1$	4	-6Dq	t_{2g}^4	2	-16Dq + P
d^5	$t_{2g}^3\ e_g^2$	5	0	t_{2g}^5	1	-20Dq + 2P
d^6	$t_{2g}^4\ e_g^2$	4	-4Dq + P	t_{2g}^6	0	-24Dq + 3P
d^7	$t_{2g}^5\ e_g^1$	2	-8Dq + 2P	$t_{2g}^6\ e_g^1$	1	-18Dq + 3P
d^8	$t_{2g}^6\ e_g^2$	2	-12Dq + 3P	$t_{2g}^6\ e_g^2$	2	-12Dq + 3P
d^9	$t_{2g}^6\ e_g^3$	1	-6Dq + 4P	$t_{2g}^6\ e_g^3$	1	-6Dq + 4P
d^{10}	$t_{2g}^6\ e_g^4$	0	0	$t_{2g}^6\ e_g^4$	0	0

6.10 Evidences for Crystal Field Stabilization Energy

The CFSE plays an important role in the thermodynamic properties of transition metal compounds.

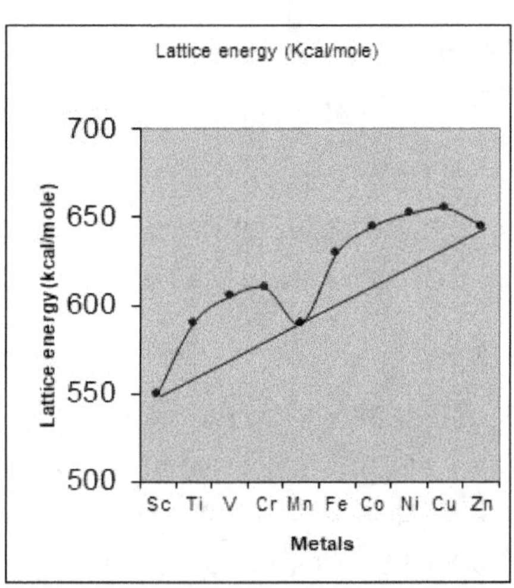

Figure 6.6: Lattice energy of the dichloride of the elements from Ca to Zn.

Many complexes of the transition metals are stabilized due to CFSE. Transition metal compounds and transition metal complexes with d^0, d^5 and d^{10} ions have no CFSE. These compounds show regular gradation in properties like lattice energy and heat of hydration. However, transition metal compounds having configuration other than d^0, d^5 and d^{10} show irregularities in these properties. Figure 6.6 shows a graph of lattice energies of the dichloride of the metals from calcium to zinc. Similar graph is for heat of hydration of various divalent ions.

The observed energies are shown by circular points in these graphs. It is seen that a smooth curve which is almost a straight line passes through the points for the three ions Ca^{+2} (d^0), Mn^{+2} (d^5) and Zn^{+2} (d^{10}) which have no CFSE while the points for all other ions lie above this line. On subtracting the CFSE from each of the actual lattice energy or heat of hydration, we will get the points which will fall on the smooth curve. These observations provide evidence for the CFSE.

6.11 Crystal Field Spectra and Measurement of $10D_q$ or Δ_0

Study of the absorption spectra of complexes enables us to find the value of $10D_q$ or Δ_0. A band or bands in the absorption spectra can be related to the excitation of an electron or electrons between d orbitals (d-d transition) split by the crystal field. The ability to interpret such spectroscopic evidence is one of the advantages of CFT.

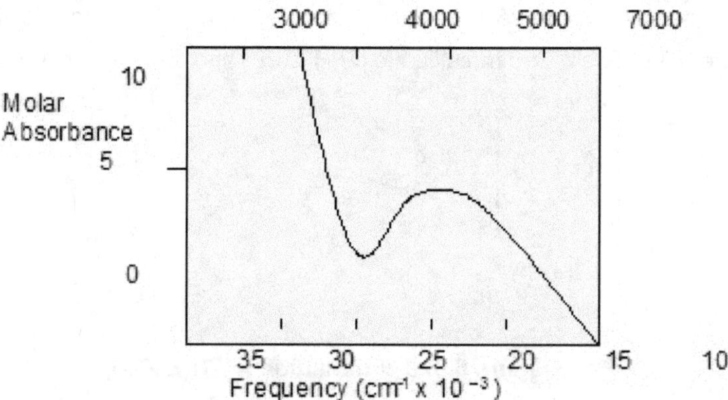

Figure 6.7: The visible absorption spectrum of $[Ti(H_2O)_6]^{+3}$ complex ion.

Let us consider the octahedral complex ion $[Ti(H_2O)_6]^{+3}$. It offers a simple case i.e. it has only one d electron. In the ground state, the electron will occupy one of the t_{2g} orbitals, but absorption of radiation will excite it into one of the e_g orbitals. Thus for d^1 ion only one transition t_{2g} to e_g is expected. The difference in energy between t_{2g} and e_g is $10D_q$ or Δ_0. Figure 6.7 shows absorption band due to d $\rightarrow$ d transition in the $[Ti(H_2O)_6]^{+3}$ complex ion.

The absorption band shows a maximum at 20400 cm^{-1} (4900 A^0)

Energy = $h\nu$ = $hc\bar{\nu}$

h = 6.624 x 10 $^{-34}$ Js molecule $^{-1}$ (plank's constant)

c = 3 x 10 ^{10} cm s $^{-1}$ (velocity of light)

$\bar{\nu}$ = 20400 cm $^{-1}$

Substituting these values we get,

Energy = 10 Dq = Δ_0

$$= 6.624 \times 10^{-34} \times 3 \times 10^{10} \times 20400$$

$$= 4.054 \times 10^{-19} \text{ Js molecule}^{-1}$$

To find out energy per mole, we multiply by Avogadro's number

= 4.054 x 10 $^{-19}$ x 6.624 x 10 $^{-34}$ J mole $^{-1}$

= 244.2 KJ mole $^{-1}$

= 58.35 K cal. Mole $^{-1}$

Thus, Δ_0 = 244.2 KJ mole $^{-1}$ = 58.35 K cal. Mole $^{-1}$

Light of frequency 20400 cm^{-1} is green. If such a light is absorbed, the transmitted light appears violet. Hence, the $[Ti(H_2O)_6]^{+3}$ ion appears violet. Figure 6.8 shows d $\rightarrow$ d transition in $[Ti(H_2O)_6]^{+3}$ and the value to 10Dq.

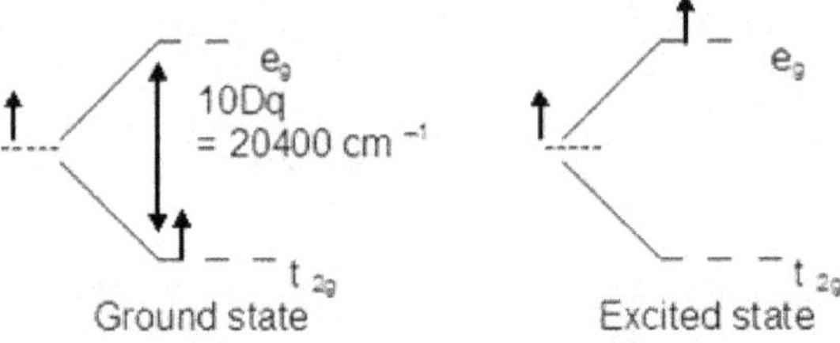

Figure 6.8: d-d transition in $[Ti(H_2O)_6]^{3+}$

With complexes containing more than one d electron. The transition and energy changes between d orbitals becomes more complex and the resulting absorption spectra contain more than one band.

6.12 Factors affecting the Magnitude of $10D_q$ or Δ_0

The magnitude of $10D_q$ or Δ_0 in an octahedral complex depend upon following three factors.

i)   Nature of the ligands.

ii)   Charge on the metal ion.

iii)   The row in which the transition metal is placed.

i) Nature of the ligands: crystal field splitting by various ligands are shown in table 6.4.

Table 6.4: Crystal field splitting by various ligands with Chromium metal

Complex ion	Absorption peak cm^{-1}	Δ_0 KJ mole^{-1}
$[CrCl_6]^{-3}$	13640	163
$[Cr(H_2O)_6]^{3+}$	17830	213
$[Cr(NH_3)_6]^{3+}$	21680	259
$[Cr(CN)_6]^{3-}$	26280	314

The value of Δ_0 increases with increasing strength of the ligand. Thus the cyanide ligand produces more splitting and is a strong ligand while chlorine produces less splitting and is a weak ligand. This forms the basis of the spectrochemical series.

ii) The charge on the metal ion:

As CFT is based on the electrostatic model, the charge on the metal ion has a direct effect on the magnitude of 10Dq.

a) Different charges on the cations of same metal:

A metal ion with high charge, attracts the ligand more close and therefore, produces more splitting than an ion with less charge.

$$e.g.\ [Cr(H_2O)_6]^{2+}\ 10Dq = 39.7\ Kcal\ mole^{-1}$$

and for $[Cr(H_2O)_6]^{3+}$ 10Dq = 50.94 Kcal mole^{-1}

Thus, higher charge (i.e. higher ox. no.) on the metal can polarize the ligands more effectively and so the ligands can approach more closely to the metal ion which will result in a greater splitting.

b) Different charges on the cations of different metal:

Two different cations with same electronic configuration and the same geometry of the complex are considered, it observed that the cation with higher charge (i.e. higher ox. no.) has a higher Δ_0 value. e.g. V^{2+} ion in $[V(H_2O)6]^{2+}$, Δ_0 = 12460 cm^{-1}

$$\text{For } Cr^{3+} \text{ ion in } [Cr(H_2O)6]^{3+} \text{ , } \Delta_0 = 17400 \text{ cm}^{-1}$$

Thus, higher charge (i.e. higher ox.no.) on the Cr^{3+}ion than V^{2+} ion can polarize the ligands more effectively and so the ligands can approach more closely to Cr^{3+}ion which will result in a greater splitting.

c) Same charge on cations with different electronic configuration:

In this type, the value decrease with increase of d- electrons.

e.g. $[Co (H_2O)6]^{2+}$, Δ_0 = 9300 cm^{-1} (d^7 system)

For $[Ni (H_2O)6]^{2+}$, Δ_0 = 8500 cm^{-1} (d^8 system)

iii) The row in which the transition metal is placed:

The variations in the Δ_0 according to the row in which the transition metal is placed is shown in table 6.5.

Table 6.5: The variations in the Δ_0 according to the row in which the transition metal is placed

Row	Complex ion	Δ_0 in cm^{-1}	Δ_0 in KJ mole^{-1}
I	$[Co (NH_3)_6]^{3+}$	23000	275
II	$[Rh (NH_3)_6]^{3+}$	34000	406
III	$[Ir (NH_3)_6]^{3+}$	41000	490

It follows that value of Δ_0 increases as we go down the group or from I to II to III row of transition elements. The d orbital splitting are in the order 3d < 4d < 5d. The increase is about 40 to 50 % from 3d to 4d and 20 to 30 % from 4d to 5d ions. In a period however the 10Dq value do not change much.

6.13 CFT and Magnetic Properties of Metal complexes

CFT explain the magnetic properties of transition metal complexes. Electron pairing energy determines the magnetic properties. If the crystal field is strong, electron pairing takes place to the maximum possible extent and the complex shows diamagnetism. e.g. $[Fe(CN)_6]^{-4}$ ion. If the crystal field is weak, no electron pairing takes place and the complex shows paramagnetism. e.g. $[FeF_6]^{-4}$ ion. with four unpaired electrons.

In the second and third transition series spin pairing will be much more because 10Dq is 50 to 100% larger in the later series and spin pairing energy becomes less. Heavier transition metal forms low spin complexes. With the help of CFT we can find out no. of unpaired electrons and magnetic properties. The magnetic moment μ of the complex can be determined by using spin only formula.

$$\mu = \sqrt{n(n+2)} \; BM$$

Where, n is the number of unpaired electrons.

6.14 Tetragonal Distortion of Octahedral Complexes (Jahn-Teller distortion)

The regular shape of the octahedral complex is distorted if the d orbital of the central ion are not occupied symmetrically. This occur when the t_{2g} or e_g set of orbitals contains a number of electrons which will neither completely fill nor half fill the set of orbitals. The effect of such a lack of symmetry on the geometrical shape of a complex is known as Jahn-teller effect.

Jahn Teller theorem states that, "Any non-linear molecular system in a degenerate electronic state will be unstable and will undergo some kind of distortion to lower the symmetry, remove the degeneracy and lower the energy of the system."

If the d electrons are symmetrically arranged with respect to an octahedral ligand field. They will repel all six ligands equally and a completely regular octahedral structure will be formed. The symmetrical and unsymmetrical arrangement of octahedral ligand field with all six ligands are shown in the table 6.6 and 6.7.

Table 6.6: Symmetrical arrangement of octahedral ligand field with all six ligands

d^n ion	Distribution of d electrons in		Nature of ligand field	Example
	t_{2g} set	e_g set		
d^0	↑		Strong or weak	$TiO_{2-,}$ $[TiF_{-6}]^{-2}$
d^3	↑ ↑ ↑		Strong or weak	$[Cr(H_2O)]^{3+}$
d^5	↑ ↑ ↑	↑ ↑	Weak	$[MnF_6]^{-4}$
d^6	↑↓ ↑↓ ↑↓		Strong	$[Fe(CN)_6]^{-4}$
d^8	↑↓ ↑↓ ↑↓	↑ ↑	Strong or weak	$[NiF_6]^{-4}$
d^{10}	↑↓ ↑↓ ↑↓	↑↓ ↑↓	Strong or weak	$[Zn(NH_3)_6]^{-2}$

Table 6.7: Unsymmetrical arrangement of octahedral ligand field with all six ligands

d^n ion	Distribution of d electrons in		Nature of ligand field	Example
	t_{2g} set	e_g set		
d^4	↑ ↑ ↑	↑	Weak	Cr(+II), Mn(+III)
d^7	↑↓ ↑↓ ↑	↑ ↑	Strong	Co(+II), Ni(+III)
d^9	↑↓ ↑↓ ↑↓	↑↓ ↑	Strong & weak	Cu(+II)

t_{2g} orbitals are directed in between the ligand directions, asymmetric filling of these orbitals has little effect on the stereochemistry. In contrast, the e_g orbitals cause some ligands to be repelled more than the others, resulting in significant distortion of the octahedral shape.

The two e_g orbitals are normally degenerate. But if one of these orbitals is asymmetrically filled in an octahedral environment, this degeneracy is destroyed and the two orbitals are no more equal in energy. e.g. Cu^{2+} (d^9) ion. The t_{2g} orbitals are full. Asymmetry is caused by incomplete filling of the e_g orbitals.

The three electrons in the e_g orbitals may be distributed as $(d_z^2)^1$ $(d_{x^2-y^2})^2$ or as $(d_z^2)^2$ $(d_{x^2-y^2})^1$. The symmetrical distribution $(d_z^2)^2$ $(d_{x^2-y^2})^2$ would give a regular octahedral complex but the $(d_z^2)^1$ $(d_{x^2-y^2})^2$ distribution differs by having one electron less in the d_z^2 orbital. As the orbital is directed along the z axis, the ligands on the z axis would be repelled less and drawn inwards if it contains only one electron. The resulting complex will be distorted having two short bonds along z axis and four long bonds along the x and y axis. The formation of shorter and longer bonds are shown in figure 6.9.
Alternatively, the electronic arrangement of resulting from $(d_z^2)^2$ $(d_{x^2-y^2})^1$ has the shortage of one electron in the $d_{x^2-y^2}$ orbital which is directed along the x and y axes. Thus ligands along x and y axes are repelled less. The distortion caused by such an arrangement of electrons result in a complex with four short bonds along x and y axes and two long bond along the z axis.

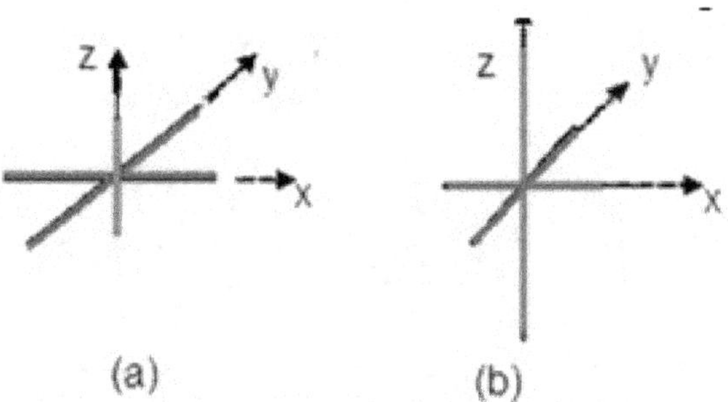

Figure 6.9: Jahn-Teller distortion a) Four long and two short bonds resulting from $(d_z^2)^1(d_{x^2-y^2})^2$ b) two longer and four shorter bonds resulting from $(d_z^2)^2(d_{x^2-y^2})^1$

There is no theoretical way of deciding which of the two possible distortion is more likely but the experimental results show that it is the arrangement of four short and two long bonds i.e. the electronic arrangement $(d_z^2)^2$ $(d_{x^2-y^2})^1$ is predominant.

In Cu(II) chloride crystal, Cu^{2+} ion is surrounded by six Cl^- ions but four of them are distance 0.23 nm, while the other two are 0.295 nm away. Such an orbital splitting is said to be tetragonal distortion. It is shown diagrammatically in figure 6.10.

Generally, 10dq >>> δ_1 > δ_2.

With reference to fig energy calculations can be done for d^9 system. The t_{2g} orbitals are fully occupied. The net stabilization energy due to t_{2g} is zero.

Net stabilization energy (t_{2g}) = [4 x (-1/3 δ_2)] + [2 x (+2/3 δ_2)

$$= o$$

The stabilization energy due to e_g orbital is

Net stabilization energy (e_g) = [2 x (-1/2 δ_1)] + [1 x (+1/2 δ_1)

$$= - 1/2\ \delta_1$$

This net energy - 1/2 δ_1 is called Jahn-Teller stabilization energy and it provides the driving force for the distortion.

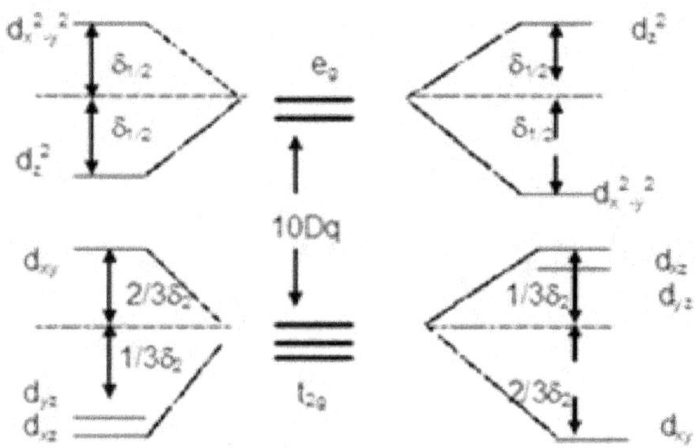

Figure 6.10: Orbital splitting with i) Ligands on z axis moving out ii) Lignads along z axis moving in for tetragonally distorted octahedral complex

6.15 Application of CFT to square planar complexes

Tetragonal distortion proceeds when ligands along z-axis go away from the central metal ion. The distortion becomes so large along z-axis are removed. This is a limiting case of tetragonal distortion.

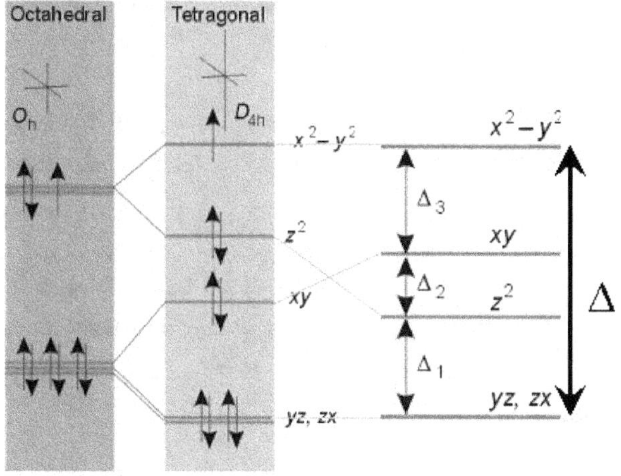

Figure 6.11: Orbital splitting leading to the ultimate formation of a square planar complex

Table 6.8: CFSE values for square planar complexes

No. of d electrons	Weak ligand field, High-spin		Strong ligand field, Low-spin	
	Unpaired e⁻	CFSE Δ_{sq}	Unpaired e⁻	CFSE Δ_{sq}
d^1	1	0.51	1	0.51
d^2	2	1.02	2	1.02
d^3	3	1.45	3	1.45
d^4	4	1.22	2	1.96
d^5	5	0.00	1	2.47
d^6	4	0.51	0	2.90
d^7	3	1.02	1	2.67
d^8	2	1.45	0	2.44
d^9	1	1.22	1	1.22
d^{10}	0	0.00	0	0.00

As a result, C.N. becomes 4 and square planar complex is formed. As the ligands along z-axis are removed the interaction of the ligands along x and y axis becomes the strongest with the $d_{x^2-y^2}$ less so with the d_{xy} and least with the d_{yz}, d_{xz} and d_{z^2} orbitals of the central metal ion.

Due to this interaction new energy differences among the d orbital of the metal ion arise. The d_{z^2} orbital becomes lower in energy & becomes more stable than the $d_{x^2-y^2}$ orbital.

At the same time, the three-fold degeneracy of the t_{2g} orbital is also removed. As the ligands on the z axis are removed, the d_{yz} and d_{xz} orbitals remain equivalent to one another but they become lower in energy and more stable than the d_{xy} orbital. This is shown in figure 6.11.

The most favorable electron configuration for square planar complexes is that of a d^8 ion. e.g. Ni^{2+}, Pt^{2+}, Pd^{2+}, Au^{3+}. In this case splitting is sufficient and pairing of electrons formed. The very high energy $d_{x^2-y^2}$ orbital is left vacant.

In square planar complexes CFSE can be calculated as follows. The orbitals are placed in such a way that the d_{xy}, d_{yz} and d_{z^2} orbitals are lowered by 0.51Δ, 0.51Δ and 0.43Δ respectively. The d_{xy} and $d_{x^2-y^2}$ orbitals are raised by 0.23Δ & 1.22Δ energies resp. table 6.8 gives CFSE values for square planar complexes.

6.16 Application of CFT to tetrahedral complexes

In tetrahedral arrangement ligand repulsion is least for a four coordinated metal ion. The radius ratio of cation to anion between 0.225 to 0.414. The four ligands in a tetrahedral complex can be considered as arranged at the alternate corners of a cube and the metal atoms at the center. The directions x, y and z points to the center of the faces of the cube. The e_g orbitals point along x, y and z that is to the center of the faces and the t_{2g} orbitals point in between x, y and z that is towards the centers of the edges of the cube.

The direction of approach of the ligands do not coincide exactly with either the e_g or the t_{2g} orbitals. The t_{2g} orbitals are nearer to the directions of the ligands than the e_g orbitals. The orientations of d orbitals in cube is shown in figure 6.12. The approach of the ligands raises the energy of the both t_{2g} and e_g sets of orbitals but since the t_{2g} orbitals are closest to the ligands their energy is raised the most. The crystal field splitting is the opposite way to that in an octahedral complex.

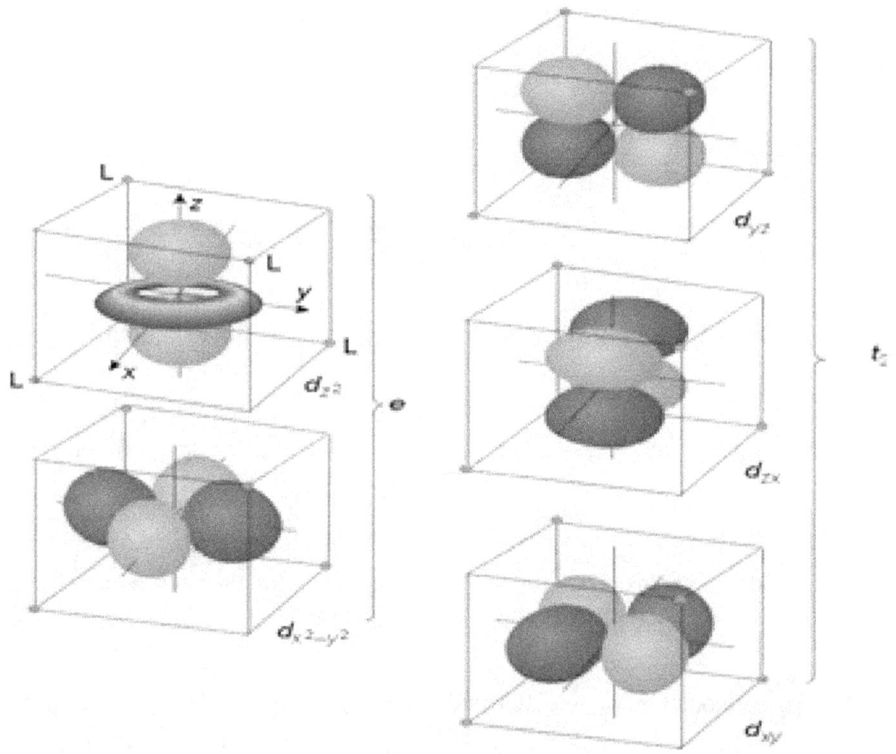

Figure 6.12: Orientation of d orbits relative to a cube

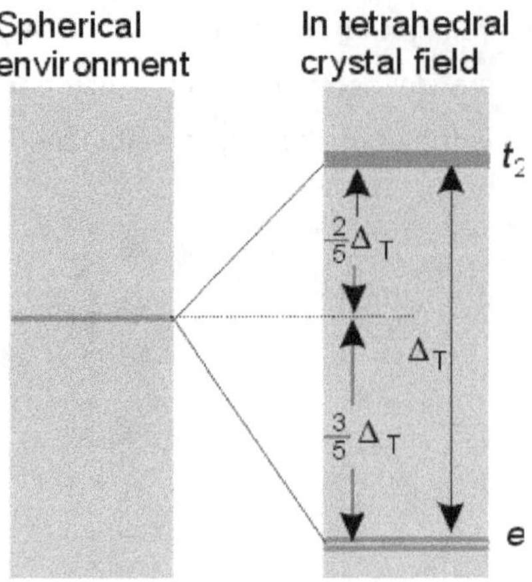

Figure 6.13: Energy levels of d orbitals in a tetrahedral field

The t_{2g} orbitals are 0.4 Δ_t above the average energy level and the e_g orbitals are 0.6 Δ_t below the average energy level. This is shown in figure 6.13. The magnitude of CF splitting Δ_t in a tetrahedral complex is less than octahedral complexes. The crystal field splitting in a is roughly 4/9th the crystal field splitting in a octahedral complex. Thus, Δ_t = 4/9 Δ_o. The difference between energy of t_{2g} & e_g is Δ_t or 10Dq.

In tetrahedral complex, the electron pairing energy is generally high. It is more than Δ_t or 10Dq. So electrons generally enter the orbitals with parallel spins. In other words tetrahedral complex are always high spin complexes. The CFSE for high spin tetrahedral & octahedral complexes are shown in table 6.9.

Table 6.9 Crystal field stabilization energies for high spin tetrahedral and octahedral configurations (other things being equal)

Number of d electrons	CFSE	
	Tetrahedral	**Octahedral**
0, 5, 10	0	
1, 6	$0.6 \, \Delta_t = 0.27 \, \Delta_o$	$0.4 \, \Delta_o$
2, 7	$1.2 \, \Delta_t = 0.53 \, \Delta_o$	$0.8 \, \Delta_o$
3, 8	$0.8 \, \Delta_t = 0.35 \, \Delta_o$	$1.2 \, \Delta_o$
4, 9	$0.4 \, \Delta_t = 0.18 \, \Delta_o$	$0.6 \, \Delta_o$

Tetrahedral complexes are favored -

1) Where the ligands are large and bulky & could cause crowding in an octahedral complex.
2) When the ligands are weak, so the loss in CFSE is less important.
3) Reduces the magnitude of Δ.

6.17 Spectrochemical series

The ligands are arranged according to their capacity to cause d orbital splitting. The magnitude of d orbital splitting is usually expressed as 10Dq or Δ. Table 6.10 shows that change in Δ_o energies when ligands were changed

Table 6.10: Crystal field splitting for some octahedral complexes with different ligands.

Complex	Δ_o cm^{-1}	Complex	Δ_o cm^{-1}
$[Ni(Br)_6]^{4-}$	7000	$[Rh(Br)_6]^{3-}$	19000
$[NiCl_6]^{4-}$	7200	$[Rh(Cl)_6]^{3-}$	20300
$[Ni(H_2O)_6]^{2+}$	8500	$[Rh(H_2O)_6]^{3+}$	27000
$[Ni(NH_3)_6]^{2+}$	10800	$[Rh(NH_3)_6]^{3+}$	34100
$[Ni(en)_3]^{2+}$	11500	$[Rh(en)_3]^{3+}$	34600

A ligand exerting a strong field gives a high Δ value and the one exerting a weak field gives a small Δ value. It is possible to list the common ligands in order of their field strength. Such a series is called spectrochemical series. It is shown as below.

$CN^- > NO_2^- > $ o-phen $ > $ dipy $ > $ en $ > NH_3 > CNS > H_2O > C_2O_4^{2-} > OH^- > F^- > Cl^- > Br^- > I^-$

6.18 Nephelauxetic effect and Nephelauxetic series

The effect of ligands in expanding the d electron cloud of the central metal ion is called the Nephelauxetic (from Greek, meaning 'cloud expanding') effect. It is believed that this expansion of the d electron cloud occurs at least partly because the metal ion d orbitals overlap with ligand atom orbitals thus providing paths by which d electrons can escape to some extent from the metal ion. This is delocalization of electrons from metal to ligand.

Common ligands are arranged in order of their ability to cause d electron cloud expansion and this series is called Nephelauxetic series. It is given below.

$$F^- < H_2O < NH_3 < C_2O_4^{2-} < \text{en} < NCS^- < Cl^- = CN^- < Br^- < I^-$$

This order is more or less independent of the metal ion. Nephelauxetic effect suggests the development of covalent bond character in a metal- ligand bond.

6.19 Limitations of CFT

1) It takes into account only the metal d orbitals and does not consider any other s and p orbitals of metal and any orbitals of ligands.
2) It considers ligands as point charges. This assumption is far from reality as creates many difficulties.
3) It does not consider the formation of covalent bonding between metal and ligand at all. There are many properties which can't be explained unless partial covalent character present in the complex.
4) It does not take into account possibility of double bond between the metal and ligand in the complexes. In practice, such a double bonding is present in some complexes.

5) The order of ligands in the spectrochemical series is defective. It can't explain why a negative ion like OH^- produce weaker field than neutral ligands like H_2O. Also, it can't explain why ligands like CO which have very low dipole moment and very low electronegativity of atoms can produce strong field.

6) Nephelauxetic effect is clearly an indication of development of covalent character in a metal- ligand bond but CFT does not explain it.

7) It can't account for back bonding in complexes.

8) It does not explain the charge transfer spectra and the intensities of the absorption band.

CHAPTER 7: MOLECULAR ORBITAL THEORY OF COORDINATION COMPLEXES

7.1 Postulates of MOT for an octahedral complex

1. The central metal ion contributes nine atomic orbitals s, p_x, p_y, p_z, $d_{x^2-y^2}$, d_{z^2}, d_{xy}, d_{yz} and d_{xz} for bonding.

2. Out of the nine orbitals, the metal ion contributes six orbitals viz. s, p_x, p_y, p_z, $d_{x^2-y^2}$ and d_{z^2} which have their lobes directed along the axis to overlap with ligand orbitals to form σ bonds.

3. Each of the six ligands contributess orbital or some combination of s – and p – orbitals, pointing towards the central metal ion to form σ bonding.

4. The six ligand orbitals combine and forms a new set of orbitals called Ligand Group Orbitals (LGOs) or Composite Ligand Orbitals. (CLOs). This set can be broken into six smaller sets of orbitals with symmetries matching to the symmetries of metal orbitals forming σ bonds.

5. Each of the metal ion orbitals combines with its matching symmetry orbital of the ligand to form σ bonding and antibonding MOs.

6. If the ligands also possesses π orbitals, they also combine to form a new set of symmetry orbitals. These ligand orbitals will then combine with metal ion orbitals of proper symmetry to form bonding and antibonding MOs.

7. The total number of electrons of the metal ion and the ligands are then filled in molecular orbitals following Aufbau principle, Hund's rule and Pauli's exclusion principle.

7.2 MO Treatment of Bonding (Octahedral complex without π Bonding)

$d_{x^2-y^2}$ and d_{z^2} orbitals together with 4s, $4p_x$, $4p_y$ and $4p_z$ combines with ligand orbitals and forms σ bonds. Molecular Orbital diagram can be prepared for different complexes between metal and ligands. The d_{xy}, d_{yz} and d_{xz} orbitals will not participate in the σ bond formation, because of unsymmetry of orbitals. Figure 7.1 shows the metal orbitals and ligand group orbitals matching in symmetry which can combine to form an octahedral complex.

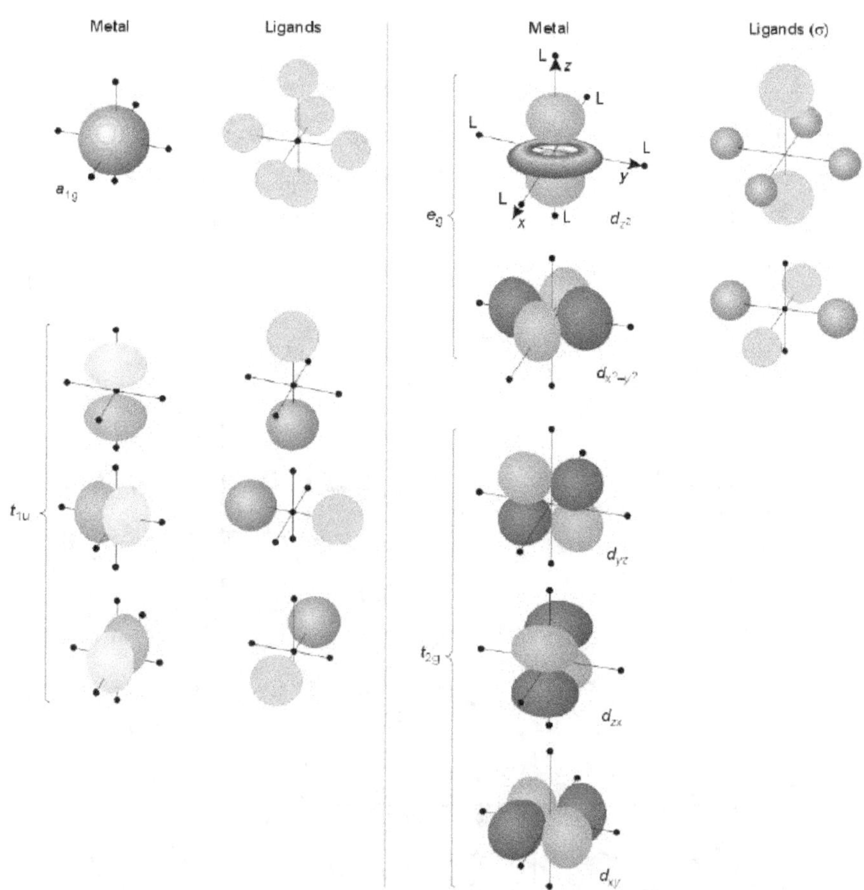

Figure 7.1: Metal matching ligand group orbitals for an octahedral complex.

For σ bonding, the ligand orbitals must lie in the direction of the lines joining the ligand and central ion. The atomic orbitals are classified according to their symmetry. The 4s orbital has a_1g symmetry, the 4p orbitals have t_1u symmetry. The ligand group orbitals break into similar sets of symmetry viz. one with a_1g symmetry, three with t_1u symmetry and two with e_g symmetry. Above figures shows that metal orbitals and ligand group orbitals matching in symmetry which can combine to form an octahedral complex.

If the six ligands are denoted as L_1, L_2, L_3, L_4, L_5 and L_6 various possible arrangements of ligand orbitals in relation to orbitals on the central ion are shown in below figure 7.2.

The ligand group orbitals could be designated as (L_1, L_2, L_3, L_4, L_5 and L_6). The ligand group orbitals, which could be symmetrical with the p_x orbital of the central ion would be (L_1-L_2). Similarly, (L_3-L_4) & (L_5-L_6) would be symmetrical with the p_y- and p_z- orbitals and (L_1+ L_2 -L_3- L_4) would be symmetrical with the $d_{x^2-y^2}$ orbitals as shown in figure 7.2.

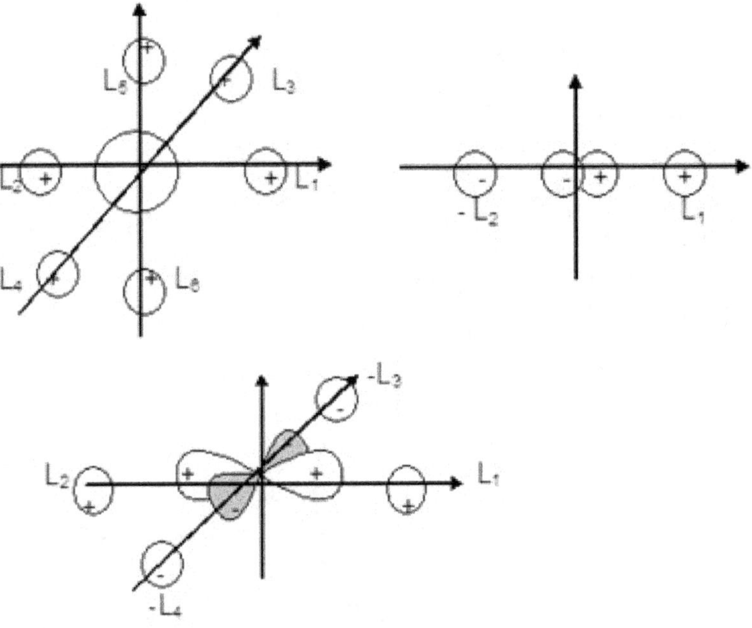

Figure 7.2: Possible combinations of orbitals of central metal ion and of the ligands s orbital, p_x orbital and $d_{x^2-y^2}$ orbital

The ligands and metal orbitals which can be combined is summarized in table 7.1.

Table 7.1: Combination of metal and ligand group orbitals

Metal orbitals	Ligand Group Orbitals
S	$L_1 + L_2 + L_3 + L_4 + L_5 + L_6$
P_x	(L_1-L_2)
p_y	(L_3-L_4)
p_z	(L_5-L_6)
$d_{x^2-y^2}$	$(L_1 + L_2 - L_3 - L_4)$
d_{z^2}	$(2L_5 + 2L_6 - L_1 - L_2 - L_3 - L_4)$

7.3 MO Energy Level Diagram

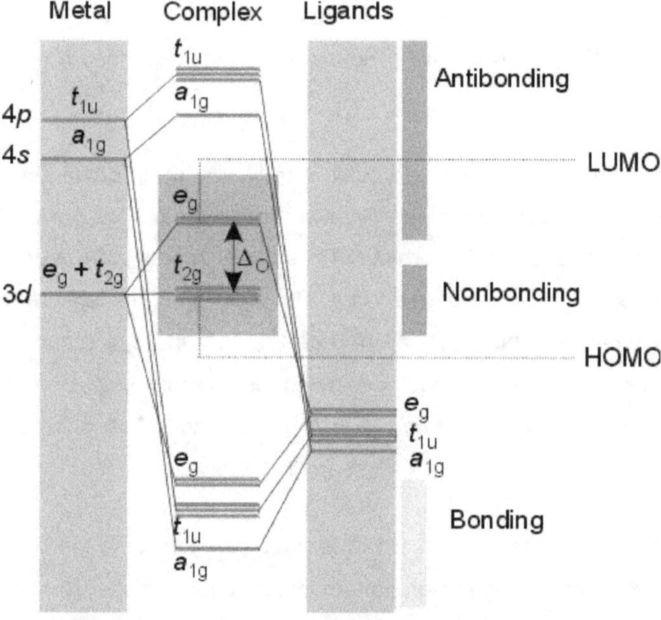

Figure 7.3: Combination of metal orbitals and ligand orbitals to form MOs in an octahedral complex.

When two atomic orbitals combine, they give two molecular orbitals. One of lower energy, is called bonding orbital and the other of higher energy, is called as an antibonding orbital. Combination of six metal orbitals and six ligand orbitals give twelve molecular orbitals. The relative energy levels are shown in the figure 7.3. The metal orbitals are shown on the left-hand side. There are in all nine metal orbitals but the three t_{2g} (d_{xy}, d_{yz} and d_{xz}) orbitals are unaffected by combination with ligand σ orbitals. The six σ orbitals of the ligands are shown on the right-hand side and the twelve molecular orbitals with the three t_{2g} orbitals are shown in the center.

The orbitals having a_{1g} symmetry give two MOs labeled as a_{1g} and $a_{1g}{}^*$. The first is bonding and other is antibonding orbital. The orbitals having t_{1u} symmetry, give six MOs. Out of them, three are called BOs which are degenerate and are labeled as t_{1u}. The remaining three are called ABOs which are degenerate and are labeled as $t_{1u}{}^*$. The orbitals having e_g symmetry give four MOs. Out of them, two are called BOs which are degenerate and are labeled as e_g. The remaining two are called ABOs which are degenerate and are labeled as $e_g{}^*$. three t_{2g} metal orbitals are unaffected so far as σ bonding is concerned, they are nonbonding orbitals.

The overlap of the metal s and p orbitals with ligand group orbitals is extensive, so there are large difference in energy between the resulting a_{1g} and $a^*{}_{1g}$ and t_{1u} & $t^*{}_{1u}$ bonding and antibonding orbitals. Thus the a_{1g} and t_{1u} BMOs are lower and $a^*{}_{1g}$ and $t^*{}_{1u}$ BMOs are highest in energy. The e_g and $e^*{}_g$ orbitals are less widely separated because of poor overlap between $d_x{}^2{}_-{}_y{}^2$ and $d_z{}^2$ orbitals and ligand group orbitals. In a system without π bonding the t_{2g} orbitals are nonbonding and therefore have the same energy as in the metal ion. The energy difference between the t_{2g} and $e^*{}_g$ MOs is called Δ_o as in CFT.

From the figure it is clear that six σ BMOs which are nearer to the ligand orbitals have more character of ligand orbitals than the metal orbitals. Hence, it can be said that the electrons occupy the BMO mainly the ligand electrons. Similarly in AMOs mainly electrons of metals are filled.

7.4 The filling of Molecular Orbitals

Electrons are filled in MOs from lower energy to higher energy as per the common electron filling rules. e.g. d^1 complex $[Ti(H_2O)_6]^{3+}$ there will be 13 electrons to be accommodated. One from titanium and twelve from the ligands. Twelve of these electrons will occupy the bonding orbitals viz. $(a_{1g})^2$, $(t_{1u})^6$ and $(e_g)^4$. There will be one electron in the t_{2g} orbital figure 7.4.

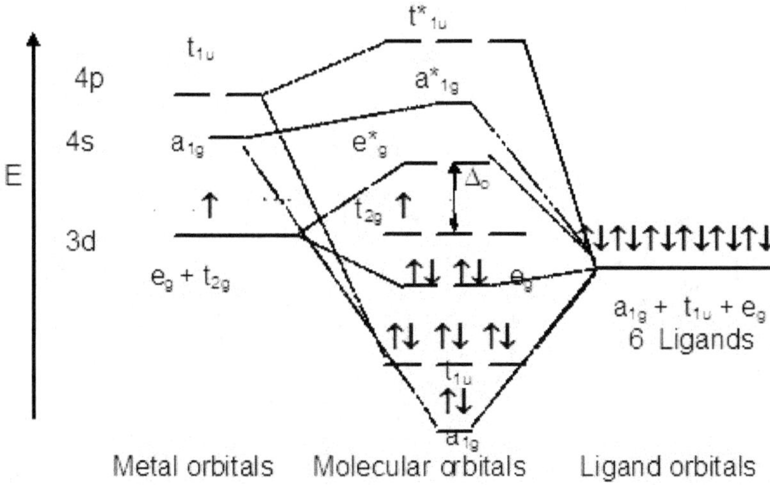

Figure 7.4: MO energy level diagram for $[Ti(H_2O)_6]^{3+}$

In d^n complexes t_{2g} & e_g orbitals will be filled as per CFT rules. Whether high or low spin complexes will be formed on the basis of value of Δ_o. The Δ_o value will be essentially the same as in CFT. The difference on this point between CFT and MOT is simply same. On the basis of CFT t_{2g} and e^*_g orbitals have different energy levels simply because of the different effect on them of an electrostatic field. On the basis of MOT, the t_{2g} and e^*_g orbitals have different energies because one set is antibonding and the other is non-bonding.

7.5 MO Energy Level Diagram of $[CoF_6]^{3-}$

Figure 7.5 show MO energy level diagram for $[CoF_6]^{3-}$. In this complex ion 18 electrons are present i.e. six from Co^{3+} ion and 12 from the ligands. Out of the 18 electrons, 12 electrons are filled in $(a_{1g})^2$, $(t_{1u})^6$ and $(e_g)^4$ orbitals from the remaining six four are filled in t_{2g} orbitals and two are placed in e^*_g orbitals. Since the energy gap between t_{2g} & e^*_g orbitals is small and pairing energy is large. Three electrons first go to t_{2g} orbitals with parallel spin, two electrons go to the e^*_g orbitals with parallel spin and then the sixth electron pairs up with one of the electrons in t_{2g} orbital. The smaller energy gap Δ_o between t_{2g} and e^*_g is attributed to the lesser extent of overlap between e_g orbitals of the metal and the ligands. Hence the $[CoF_6]^{3-}$ ion contains four unpaired electrons. It shows paramagnetism and it is high spin complex.

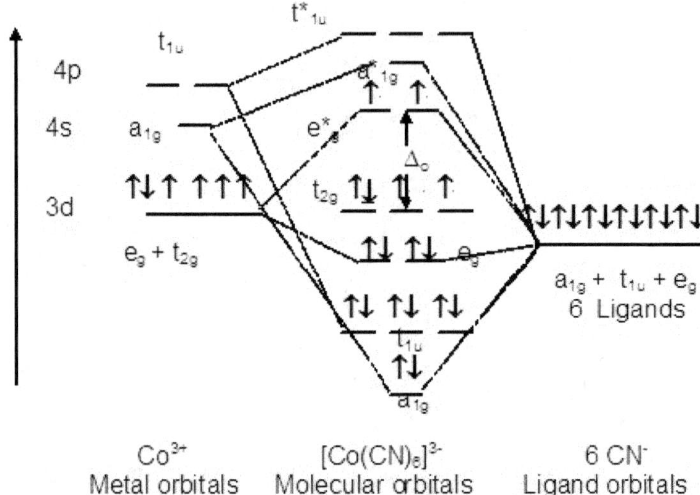

Figure 7.5: MO energy level diagram for $[Co(F)_6]^{3-}$

7.6 MO Energy Level Diagram of $[Co(CN)_6]^{3-}$

Figure 7.6 show MO energy level diagram for $[Co(CN)_6]^{3-}$. In this complex ion 18 electrons are present i.e. six from Co^{3+}ion and 12 from the ligands. Out of the 18 electrons, 12 electrons are filled in $(a_{1g})^2$, $(t_{1u})^6$ and $(e_g)^4$ orbitals from the remaining six, all six electrons are filled in t_{2g} orbitals and no any electron placed in e^*_g orbitals. Since the energy gap between t_{2g} & e^*_g orbitals is high and pairing energy is less. Hence $[Co(CN)_6]^{3-}$ ion have not any unpaired electrons. It shows diamagnetism and it is low spin complex.

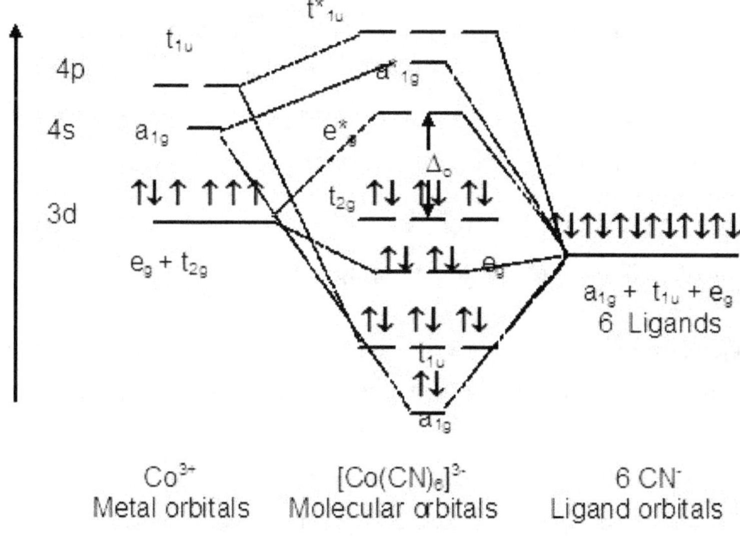

Figure 7.6: MO energy level diagram for $[Co(CN)_6]^{3-}$

7.7 MO Energy Level Diagram of $[Co(NH_3)_6]^{2+}$

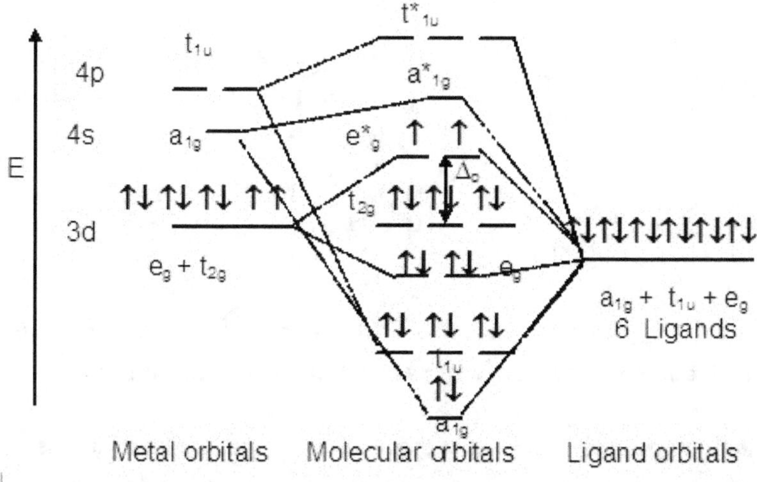

Figure 7.7: MO energy level diagram for $[Co(NH_3)_6]^{2+}$

Figure 7.7 show MO energy level diagram for $[Co(NH_3)_6]^{2+}$. In this complex ion 20 electrons are present i.e., eight from Co^{3+}ion and 12 from the ligands. Out of the 20 electrons, 12 electrons are filled in $(a_{1g})^2$, $(t_{1u})^6$ and $(e_g)^4$ orbitals from the remaining eight, six electrons are filled in t_{2g} orbitals and two electrons placed in e^*_g orbitals. Hence $[Co(NH_3)_6]^{2+}$ ion have two unpaired electrons. It shows paramagnetism.

7.8 Octahedral Complexes with π bonding

If the ligands have π orbitals, filled or unfilled, it is necessary to consider their interaction with the metal orbitals. Let us consider this simplest case where each ligand offers a pair of π orbitals, which are perpendicular to each other, for π bonding. (Usually out of the three orbitals one is used for σ bonding and the remaining two are used for π bonding). Thus, six ligands offer 6 x 2 = 12 orbitals for π bonding. Following figure7.8 show ligand π orbitals.

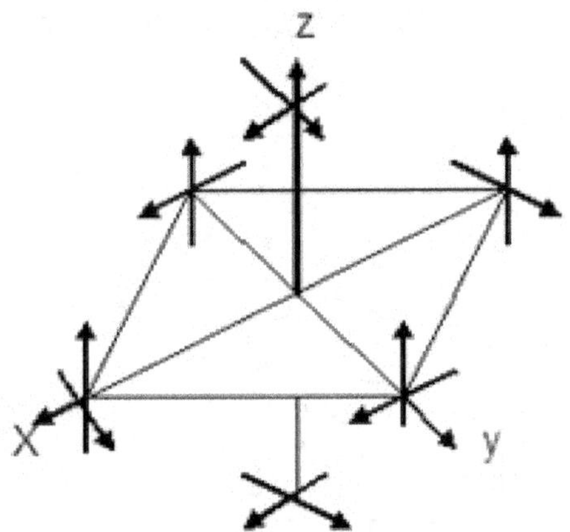

Figure 7.8: Ligand π orbitals in an octahedral complex, the arrow head represents the lobes of each orbital with positive phase

From the group theory, it is found that these may be combined into four triply degenerate sets belonging to symmetry classes t_{1g}, t_{1u}, t_{2g} and t_{2u}. There are no metal orbitals of the t_{1g} and t_{2u} symmetries. These π ligand group orbitals are, therefore, carried over, unmodified, into the full molecular orbital description.

Thus, t_{1g} and t_{2u} ligand orbital remain non-bonding, with respect to π bonding.

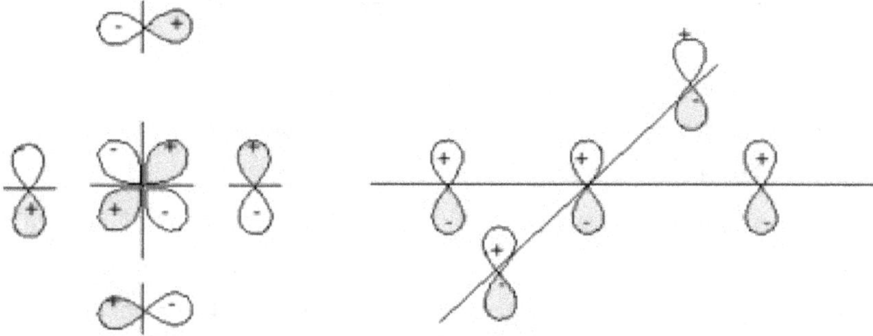

Figure 7.9:   a) Combination of metal d_{xz} b) Combination of metal p_z orbital with p_x and p_z orbital   orbital with p_z orbital of the of the ligands   ligands

The t_{1u} set of ligand group orbitals can interact with metal ion p orbital (with t_{1u} symmetry)). But the metal ion p orbitals with t_{1u} symmetry have been already used in σ bonding with ligand orbitals. So, if at all π bonding takes place between metal orbitals of t_{1u} symmetry and ligand group orbitals of t_{1u} symmetry. It will be weak. Then only t_{2g} orbitals of metal and t_{2g} orbital of ligand of same symmetry can form π bonding. Figure 7.9 (a) shows combination of metal d_{xz} orbital (t_{2g} symmetry) with p_x and p_z orbital of the ligand (t_{2g} symmetry).and fig 8(b) shows combination of metal p_z orbitals (t_{1u} symmetry).

Figure 7.10 shows splitting of t_{2g} orbitals into t_{2g} (bonding) and t^*_{2g} (antibonding) MOs due to interaction of t_{2g} metal and t_{2g} ligand orbitals. Orbitals of t_{2g} symmetry on metal and ligand.

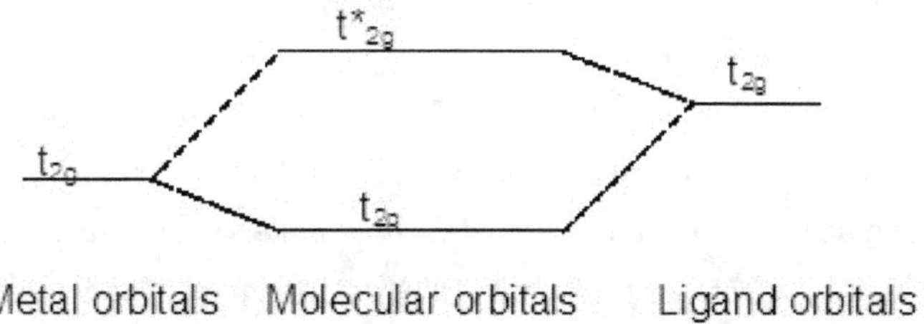

Figure 7.10: Energy level diagram for formation of MOs from π bonding

7.9 Effect of π bonding on complexes

Consider the formation of π bonding, the ligand can use its-

1) P orbitals perpendicular to the σ bond axis as in the halide ion.
2) d orbitals lying in the plane which includes the metal atom as in phosphates or arsines.
3) An antibonding π^* orbital in a plane that includes the metal atom as in Co, CN⁻, pyridine.
4) π bonding modifies the energy level diagram of a σ bonded complex, particularly the central part of the figure 7.12 where Δ_o is the difference between the t_{2g} and e^*_g orbitals.

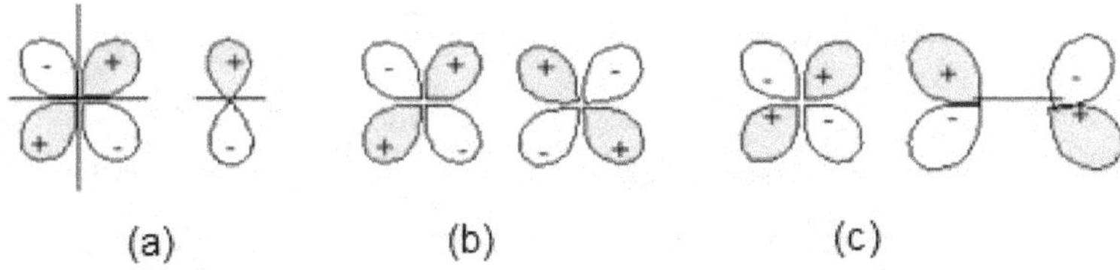

Figure 7.11: π bond formation between a metal t2g orbital and a ligand (a) p orbital (b) d orbital (c) π* orbital

7.10 Effect of π bonding on the magnitude of Δ_o

If the filled ligand orbitals lie at a lower energy than the metal t_{2g} orbital (e.g. if the ligand is a halide ion and uses its filled p orbital for π bonding), π bonding affects the energy level diagram as shown in figure 7.12.

1) Filled (donor) ligand orbitals of low energy:

In this case, the π bonding MOs resemble the ligand orbitals more than the metal orbitals. The e^*_g orbitals are not affected by π bonding. But the $\pi^*(t^*_{2g})$ molecular orbitals (originally coming from metal t_{2g} orbitals) are raised in energy subsequently. Δ_o which was originally the difference between the t_{2g} and e^*_g orbitals in a σ bonded complex, becomes the difference the between t^*_{2g} and e^*_g molecular orbitals. Since the t^*_{2g} orbitals are raised in energy with respect to t_{2g} metal orbitals, the magnitude of Δ_o is reduced. As a result, a complex is destabilized. This type of π bonding is called ligand to metal (L$\rightarrow$ M) π bonding.

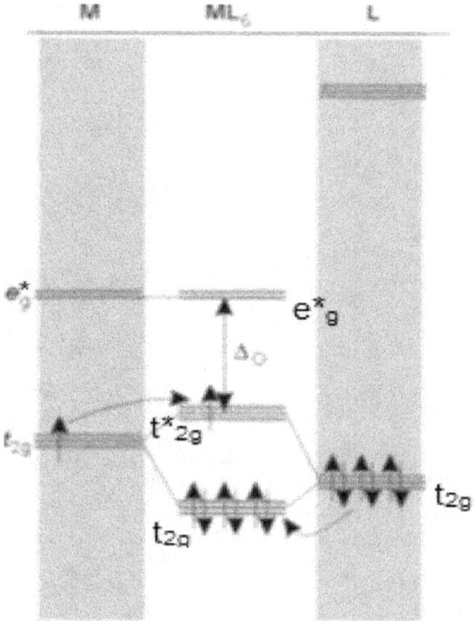

Figure 7.12: Energy level diagram showing the interaction of the t_{2g} orbital with lower energy filled orbitals of the ligands, leading to a decrease in Δ_o

2) Empty (acceptor) ligand orbitals of high energy:

If the empty ligand orbitals lie at a higher energy than the metal t_{2g} orbital (e.g. if the ligand is a phosphine and uses its empty d orbital or the ligand is carbon monoxide and uses its empty π^* molecular orbital for π bonding), π bonding affects the energy level diagram as shown in figure 7.13.

In this case, the π bonding MOs resemble the ligand orbitals more than the metal orbitals. Due to pi bonding overlap, the π (t_{2g}) level of the MOs (originally coming from metal t_{2g} orbitals) gets lowered in energy in the complex, the e^*_g orbitals are not affected by π bonding. While $\pi^*(t^*_{2g})$ level (originally coming from metal t_{2g} orbitals) is raised above the ligand orbitals.

Subsequently, Δ_o which was originally the difference between the t_{2g} and e^*_g orbitals is increased. As a result, a complex is stabilized. This type of π bonding is called metal to ligand (M → L) π bonding. In this case electronic charge is removed from central metal to the ligands. This is called back donation or back bonding.

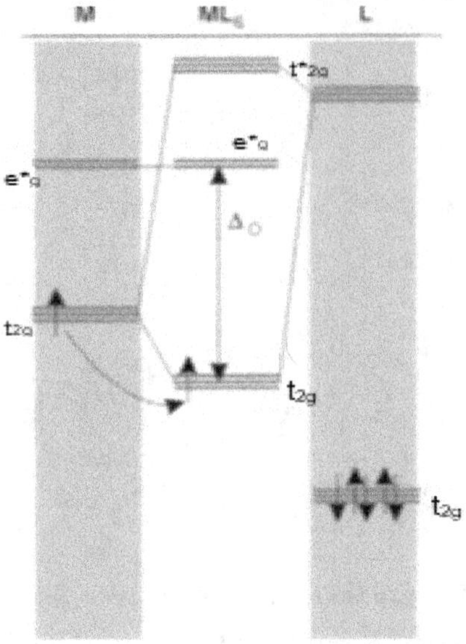

Figure 7.13: Energy level diagram showing the interaction of the t$_{2g}$ orbital with higher energy empty orbitals of the ligands, leading to a increase in Δ$_o$

7.11 Ligand Field Theory

Van Vleck developed this theory between 1939 and 1940. The CFT treats the interaction between the metal ion and ligands as a purely electrostatic problem in which the ligand atoms are represented as point charge. At the opposite extreme, so to speak, the metal ligand interaction can be described in terms of MOs formed by the overlap of ligand and metal orbitals. These two approaches use different physical interpretation of the problem but both use symmetry properties of the complex. The basic difficulty with the CFT treatment is that it takes no account of the partly covalent nature of the metal- ligand bonds and therefore, whatever effects and phenomena arise directly from covalence are entirely unexplainable in simple CFT. On the other hand CFT can provide a very simple and easy way to treat numerically many aspects of the electronic structure of complexes. MOT, in contrast, does not provide numerical results in such an easy way. Therefore, a kind of modified CFT has been developed in which certain parameters are empirically adjusted to allow for the effects of covalence without introducing covalence into the CFT formalism. This modified CFT is called Ligand Field theory.

7.12 Charge Transfer Spectra

Absorption of light takes place to cause electronic transition within as atom or molecule, it is essential that the absorption results in a displacement of charge density. The displacement of charge density may take place within an atom (d-d transition) or the displacement of the charge density may takes place from one atom to another, we call it as charge transfer transition.

The CFT can't explain the charge transfer transition because it does not take covalent bonding into account. MO treatment is necessary to explain charge transfer transition. Thus, when the absorption of radiation causes an electronic transition between two MOs such that one MO is more concentrated at one atom while the other MO is more concentrated on a different atom we call it a charge transfer transition. And the graph of absorption versus wavelength of light as a charge transfer band or spectrum. For transition metal complexes the charge transfer bands occur in the UV region. They are generally far more intense than the d $\rightarrow$ d bands. Charge transfer bands can be classified into two groups.

i) Ligand $\rightarrow$ Metal (Reduction) Transition:

These are a common type of transition in which a ligand electron is transferred to a metal orbital and the charge separation within the complex is thereby reduced. In these transitions the electrons from BMOs are excited to the empty t_{2g} or e^*_g MOs. Such charge transfer bands are shown by the oxides, chlorides, bromides etc. the dark colour of $[CuCl_4]^{2-}$, the yellow colour of $[FeCl_6]^{3-}$ is due to charge transfer transition.

ii) Metal $\rightarrow$ Ligand (Oxidation) Transition:

In these transitions, an electron is transferred to a metal orbital to ligand orbital. In such transitions, the electrons from σ BMOs are excited to the empty π MOs localized predominantly on ligands. Such charge transfer bands are shown by the CO, CN⁻, NO ligands. The Metal → Ligand charge transfer also occur in the red complexes of iron (+II) with dipyridyl or o-phenanthroline. This transition is favored if the metal is in a low oxidation state and the ligand has a low-lying antibonding orbital.

CHAPTER 8: MOLECULAR ORBITAL THEORY OF COVALENT BONDING

8.1 VALENCE BOND THEORY

The theory was developed by Hitler and London in 1927 and later extended by Pauling and Slater in 193.The theory is based on the following two principles.

(i) If ψA and ψB are the wave function for two isolated independent atoms A and B, then the total wave function ψ of the system can be written as a product of the wave functions of the two atoms.

$$\psi = \psi A \cdot \psi B$$

(ii) If a system can be represented by wave functions such as ψ_1, ψ_2, ψ_3 ----, then the true wave function ψ can be obtained by taking a linear combination of all these wave functions.

$$\psi = N (C_1 \psi_1 + C_2 \psi_2 + C_3 \psi_3 + \text{-------})$$

Where, N is the normalization constant and C_1, C_2, C_3 ----- are the various coefficients. These Coefficients are so adjusted as to give a state of lowest energy and maximum stability. The assumptions of valence bond approach based on the above principles may be given as follows.

1)   Atoms maintain their individuality in a molecule.

2) The bond is formed due to interaction of valence electron as the atom approach each other.

3) When bond is formed between the atoms, only one electron from each bonded atom loses its identity.

4) The electrons forming the bond between the two atoms undergo exchange between them and thus bond is stabilized.

8.2 Main features of valence bond theory

1) Overlapping of atomic orbitals of the two atoms having unpaired electron forms bond and electron spins are mutually neutralized.

2) The electron pair is localized between the two bonded atoms.

3) Strength of the bond depends on the extent of overlapping. Larger the area of overlap, stronger is the bond formed.

4) It gives explanation for the presence of partial ionic nature in a covalent bond.

5) It introduced the concept of resonance and the connection between resonance energy and molecular stability.

8.3 Molecular Orbital Theory (M.O.T.)

This theory put forward by Hund and Mulliken. It treats the molecule in the same way as an atom.   It is based on following assumption.

1) A molecule is made of atoms.

2) When a molecule is formed, atoms lose their individual character.

3) A molecular orbital is associated with a molecule as a whole.

4) Electrons in molecule are delocalized as compared to what they are in an isolated atom.

5) The quantised molecular orbitals of varying energy levels surround all the nuclei of the bonded atoms.

6) A molecular orbital is associated to be formed by the coalescence of the individual atomic orbitals when the atoms to be bonded come together.

7) The wave functions of a molecular orbital are obtained by linear combination of wave functions of atomic orbitals.

8.4 Comparison of V.B Theory and M.O. Theory

1) The valence bond theory considers an atom consisting of a nucleus and electrons present in an atomic orbital. Thus the atomic orbital is monocentric. The molecular orbital theory considers that an electron in a molecule moves in the field of more than one nucleus and one or more than one nucleus. Thus, the molecular orbital is polycentric.

2) Just as there are atomic orbitals s, p, d and f in an atom, there are molecular orbitals σ, л, δ in a molecule.

3) Just as there are atomic orbitals possess different shapes and energies, molecular orbital possesses different shapes and energies.

4) Just as there are atomic orbitals can be arranged in their increasing order of energy, the molecular orbital can also be arranged in the increasing order of energy.

5) Just as ϕ denotes the electron density in a particular orbital of an atom, Ψ denotes the electron density in a particular molecular orbital.

6) Just as we use aufbau principle for atoms, we can use it for molecule. Therefore, (a) each molecular orbital can accommodate two electrons with opposite spins and (b) the electrons are first filled into the lower energy orbital then the electron go to the higher energy available molecular orbital one at a time.

7) The atomic orbital of two or more atoms combine to form a molecular orbital only when they have i) close distance ii) similar energy iii) matching symmetry iv) matching geometry.

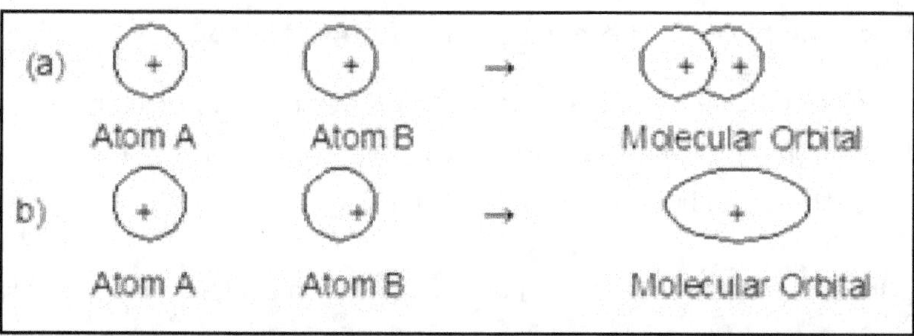

Figure 8.1: Formation of a molecular orbital by VBT and MOT

8) Figure 8.1 (a) shows that when A and B combine, they do not lose their identity while forming a molecular orbital by V.B.Theory. Figure 8.1(b) shows that when A and B combine, they lose their identity while forming a molecular orbital by M.O. Theory. Table 8.1 represents the comparison between atomic orbital and molecular orbital.

Table 8.1: Comparison of Atomic Orbital and Molecular Orbital

Atomic Orbital	Molecular Orbital
1. It contains a single nucleus i.e. it is monocentric	1. It contains more than two nucleus i.e. it is polycentric.
2. Nucleus of the atom is fixed in Space.	2. Nucleus of the constituent atoms of the molecule are Fixed in space at their proper relative orientation.
3. They are named as s, p, d and f.	3. They are named as σ, π and δ.
4. It is derived from a particular atom.	4. It is derived from the constituent atoms.
5. It has a definite shape, size and energy.	5. The shape, size and energy of a M.O. depends upon the shape, size and energy of orbital of constituent atoms.

8.5 Linear Combination of Atomic Orbitals (LCAO) Method

It is a simple and useful method of obtaining a wave function, which is described as follows: Consider two similar atoms H and H. These atoms with their atomic orbitals are described by some wave function say ϕ_1 and ϕ_2.

When these atoms form a bond the electrons in the atomic orbitals occupy molecular orbitals. The molecular orbital is formed by linear combination of the atomic orbitals ϕ_1 and ϕ_2 that is, by adding or subtracting the two wave functions.

$$\Psi = \phi_1 \pm \lambda \phi_2$$

Where, Ψ is the wave function of the molecular orbital, ϕ_1 and ϕ_2 are the wave functions of atomic orbitals of atom A and B and λ is the mixing coefficient which is the measure of ionic character of the bond formed between atom 1 and 2. For a homonuclear diatomic molecule, that is, where atoms 1 and 2 are identical, λ is equal to 1 and wave function of the molecular orbital is written as

$$\Psi = \phi_1 \pm \phi_2$$

Let us take an example of H_2 molecule. The hydrogen molecule is formed by combination of two hydrogen atoms. Let us consider that ϕ_1 and ϕ_2 represents the wave function of atomic orbital 1s for hydrogen atom 1 and 2. Then there are two possible ways of combination of the wave function ϕ_1 and ϕ_2.

1. In one way of combination, the signs of the two wave functions are same and in the other way of combination the signs of the two wave function are different.
2. The signs (+) and (-) refer to the sign of the wave functions. These signs determine the symmetry of the wave function. (The signs should not be confused with the signs of the charged bodies).

A wave function Ψ describes the probability of finding the electron and Ψ^2 describes the electron density. Wave functions, which have the same sign, may be considered as waves that are in phase, which then combined add up to give a larger resultant wave as shown in figure 8.2.

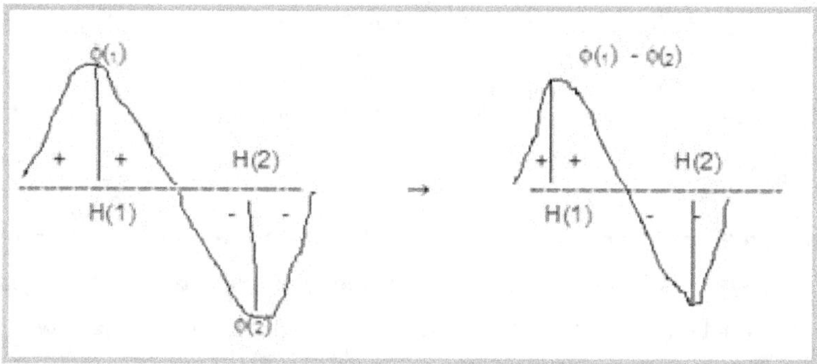

Figure 8.2: Combination of the wave functions of AOs having the same sign, waves in phase

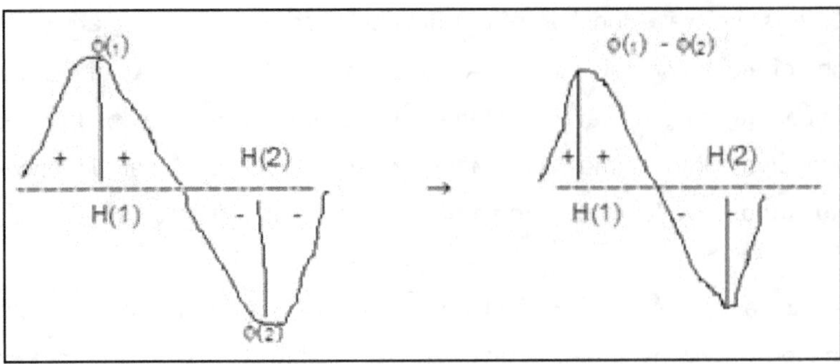

Figure 8.3: Combination of the wave functions of AOs having the different sign, waves that are out of phase

Similarly, wave functions of different signs, correspond to wave that are completely out of phase and which cancel each other by destructive interface, as shown in figure 8.3. Figure 8.2 and 8.3 show a graph of probability of electron as a function of internuclear distance. The two ways of combination are

$$\Psi\,(g) = \phi_1 + \phi_2 \quad \text{------- (2)}$$
$$\Psi\,(u) = \phi_1 + (\,-\phi_2\,) \quad \text{------- (3)}$$

Equation 3 should be considered as the summation of the wave functions and not as the mathematical difference between them.

Thus, when a pair of atomic orbitals ϕ_1 and ϕ_2 combine, they produce a pair of MOs $\Psi(g)$ and $\Psi(u)$. Hence the number of MOs produced must always be equal to the number of AOs taking part in combination. That is, orbitals are not destroyed. Such type of addition and subtraction of wave functions of the AOs is termed as LCAO principle. In the MO theory, wave functions are designated as $\Psi(g)$ and $\Psi(u)$.

The **letter g stands for gerade (even)** and the **letter u stands for ungerade (odd).** The symbols g and u refer to the symmetry of the orbital about its center. The wave function is gerade, if the sign of Ψ remains unchanged, when the orbital is reflected about its center. The wave function is ungerade, if the sign of Ψ changed, when the orbital is reflected about its center. (i.e. x, y and z are replaced by –x, -y, and –z). The symmetry of the M.O. is also determined by another method. In this method, the molecular orbital is first rotated about the line joining the two nuclei and then rotated about a line perpendicular to the inter nuclear axis. The MO is gerade, if the sign of the lobes remains the same and the orbital is ungerade, if the sign changes.

The function $\Psi(g)$ leads to increased electron density in between the nuclei and is, therefore, a Bonding Molecular Orbital (BMO) (attraction between the atoms). On the other hand, the wave functions $\Psi(u)$ leads to decreased electron density, that is, zero electron density in between the nuclei. This therefore an Anti-Bonding Molecular Orbital (ABMO) (repulsion between the atoms). The ABMO is higher in energy and is indicated by *. The BMO is lower in energy. The gerade orbital Ψ (g) hereafter will be indicated by the symbol Ψ meaning thereby a bonding MO and the ungerade orbital $\Psi(u)$ hereafter will be indicated by the symbol Ψ^* meaning thereby an antibonding MO.

The electron distribution in a MO can be obtained by squaring the wave function. On squaring equation 2 and 3, we get

$$\Psi^2_g = \phi_1{}^2 + \phi_2{}^2 + 2\,\phi_1\,\phi_2 \text{ -------------- (4)}$$
$$\Psi^2_u = \phi_1{}^2 + \phi_2{}^2 - 2\,\phi_1\,\phi_2 \text{ -------------- (5)}$$

Equation (4) and (5) represent the probability functions for bonding Ψ and antibonding Ψ^* MOs respectively. These two MOs differ by $2\,\phi_1\,\phi_2$. The wave function $\phi_1 + \phi_2$ increases the electron density in between the nuclei by the amount $2\,\phi_1\,\phi_2$ and is, therefore, a bonding MO.

The wave functions $\phi_1 - \phi_2$ decreases the electron density in between the nuclei by an amount $2\,\phi_1\,\phi_2$ and is therefore, an antibonding MO.

8.6 Formation of Bonding and Antibonding MOs (Pictorial representation)

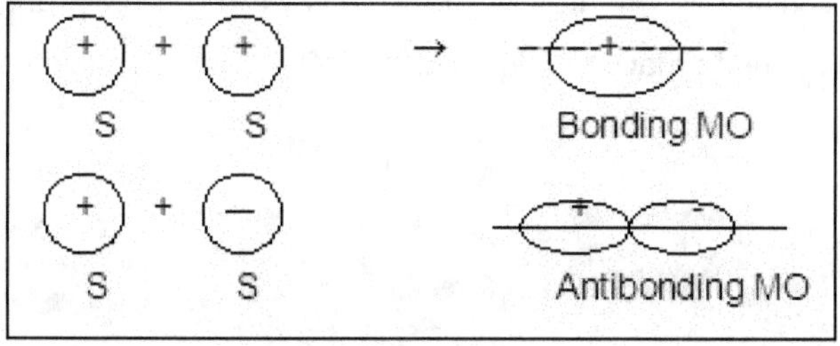

Figure 8.4: Formation of bonding and antibonding Mos

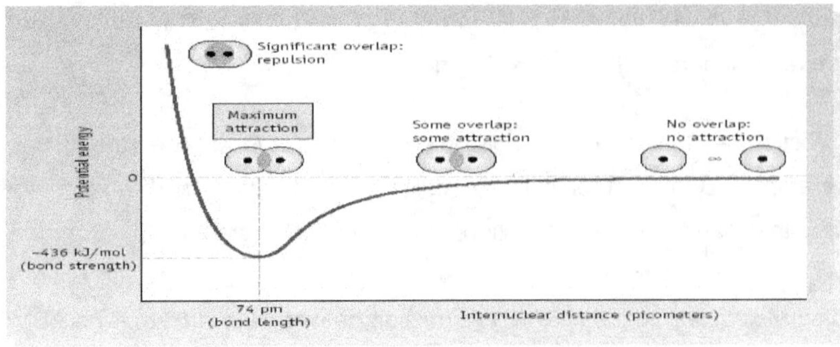

Figure 8.5: Energy diagram of sigma bond formation by orbital overlap

Two atomic orbitals (say 1s) combine to give a pair of MOs Ψ bonding and Ψ^* antibonding. The overlap of atomic orbital along the axis joining the nuclei forms a σ bond so these molecular orbital are further called σ bonding MOs and σ^* antibonding MOs. Figure 8.4 shows formation of bonding and antibonding MOs. Figure 8.5 shows energy level diagram of sigma bond formation by orbital overlap.

8.7 M.O. Energy Level Diagram

When two 1S orbitals combine, they form a Ψ (or σ) MO and a Ψ^*(or σ^*) MO. Figure 8.6 shows the energy level of atomic orbitals and molecular orbitals. In this diagram, the AOs are shown to the sides and the molecular orbitals formed are shown in the center. The two AOs ϕ_1 and ϕ_2 are of identical energy and hence the MOs Ψ and Ψ^* or σ and σ^* contain equal contribution from ϕ_1 and ϕ_2. The MO energy level diagram is symmetrical. The energy evolved during the formation of bonding MO, that is, Ψ or σ is shown as $-\Delta$ or $-\beta$ and the energy absorbed during the formation of antibonding MO, Ψ^*or σ^* is shown as $+\Delta$ or $+\beta$.

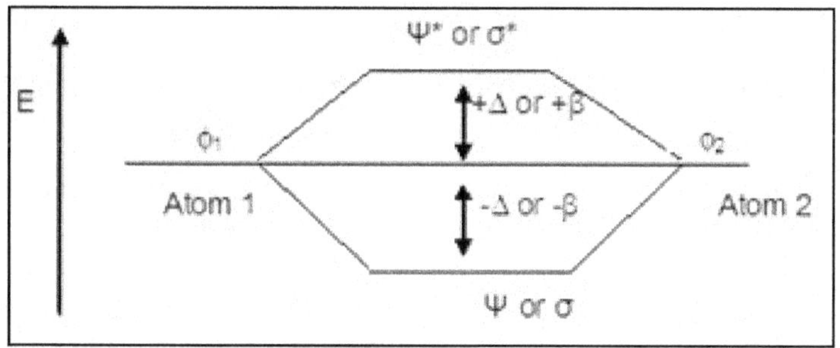

Figure 8.6: MO Energy level diagram after combination of two 1s orbitals

The energy of bonding MO is lower than that of the AO by an amount Δ or β known as **stabilization energy**. Similarly, the energy of antibonding MO is greater than that of the AO by an amount Δ or β known as **destabilization energy**.The decrease in energy is balanced by the increase in energy.

8.8 Comparison between Bonding MO and Antibonding MO

Table 8.2 shows difference between bonding molecular orbital and antibonding molecular orbital.

Table 8.2 Bonding molecular orbital and antibonding molecular orbital

BMO	ABMO
1. It is obtained by addition of wave Function of AOs.	1. It is obtained by subtraction of wave function of AOs.
2. It has lower energy than that of combining AOs.	2. It has higher energy than that of combining AOs.
3. It is stable.	3. It is unstable.
4. Electron density is Concentrated In the region between the nuclei.	4. Electron density is away from Internuclear region.
5. It results in bonding.	5. It results in non-bonding.
6. Nuclear repulsion is shielded.	6. Nuclear repulsion is not shielded.
7. There is no node.	7. It has a node perpendicular to the bond axis.

8.9 Combination of s-s, s-p, p-p, p-d and d-d orbitals

8.9.1 Combination of s and s atomic orbitals

In this case, s orbital of one atom combines with the s orbital of the other atom. This forms an σ bond and hence the σ MOs. This is shown in Figure 8.7.

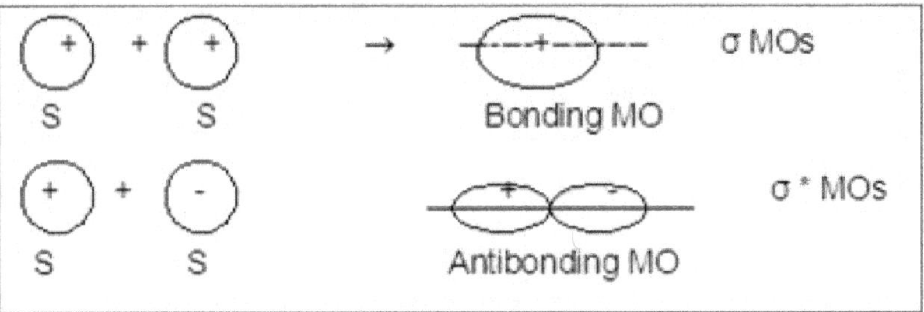

Figure 8.7: Formation of σ bond by s-s overlap

8.9.2 Combination of s and p atomic orbital

S orbital of one atom may combine with p orbital of the other atom. This combination takes place only when lobes of the p-orbital are pointing along the axis joining the nuclei. This forms σ bond and hence the σ MOs. It is shown in Figure 8.8.

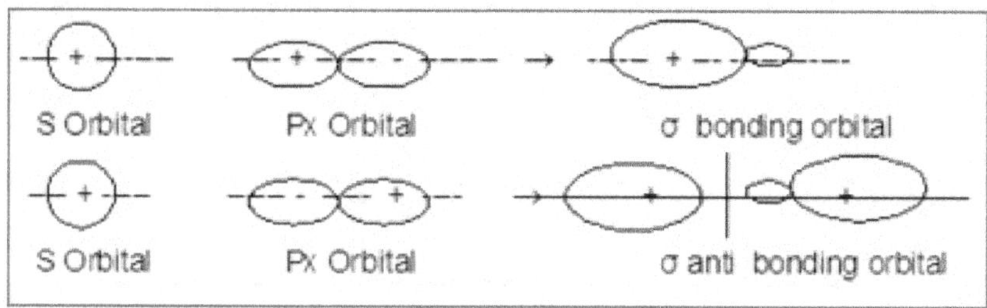

Figure 8.8: Formation of σ bond by s- p overlap

8.9.3 Combination of p and p atomic orbitals

The combination of p-orbital of one atom with the p-orbital of the other atom is called p-p combination. Overlapping of AOs produces MOs.

8.9.3.1 Formation of σ - MOs

Let us first consider the combination of two p-orbitals both of which have lobes pointing along the axis joining the nuclei. This forms an σ bond and hence the σ MOs. This produces a bonding MO and an antibonding MO, as shown in Figure 8.9.

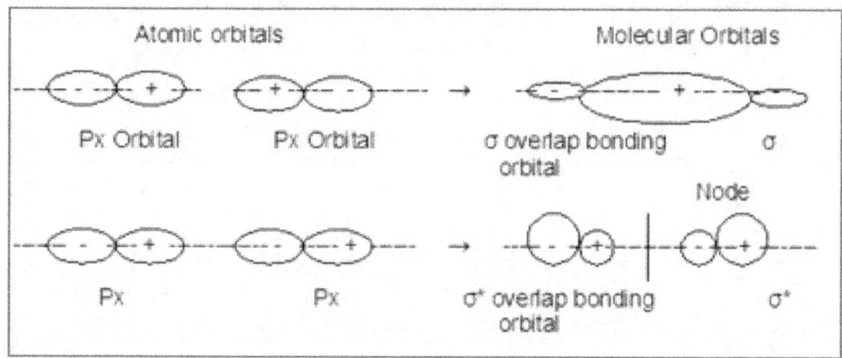

Figure 8.9: p-p combination of orbitals

Here X-axis has been assumed to be the molecular axis.

8.9.3.2 Formation of π MOs

Consider the combination of two p- orbitals both of which have lobes perpendicular to the axis joining the nuclei. This forms a π bond and hence π MOs. Lateral overlap of orbitals occur. This produces π bonding and π antibonding MOs, as shown in figure 8.10.

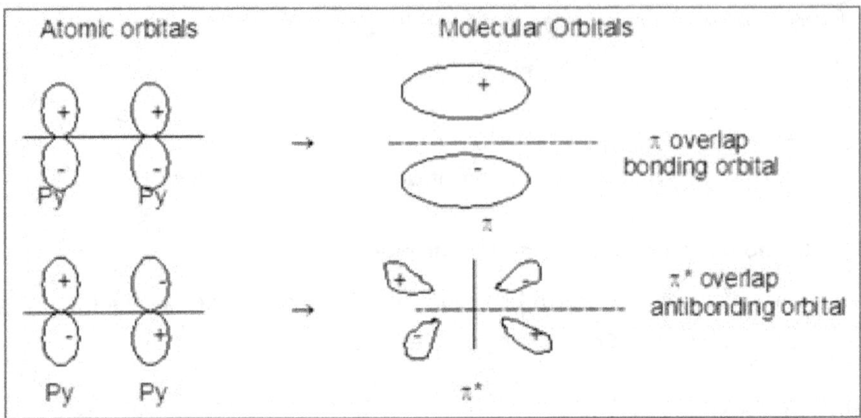

Figure 8.10: Combination p-p atomic orbitals giving π bonding and antibonding molecular orbitals

Difference between σ and π MOs:

Table 8.3 represents the difference between σ Mos and π Mos.

Table 8.3 σ Mos and π MOs

σ MOs	π MOs
1. Formed by the overlap of the lobes of AOs pointing along the internuclear line.	1. Formed by the overlap of the lobes of AOs perpendicular to the line Joining to the nuclei.
2. The electron density is concentrated between the two nuclei.	2. The electron density is zero between the two nuclei.
3. All bonding MOs are symmetric about the internuclear axis. All σ antibonding MOs are unsymmetric.	3. These have no symmetry about the internuclear axis. All π antibonding MOs are symmetric.

8.9.3.3 Combination of p and d atomic orbitals

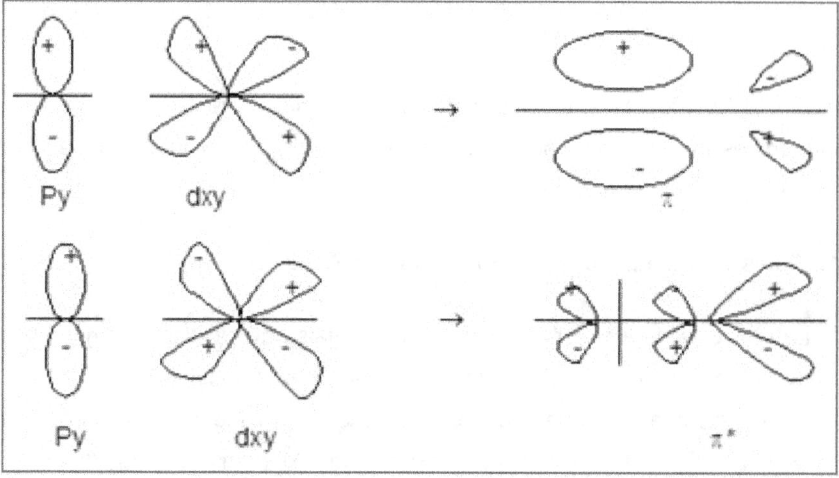

Figure 8.11: Combination of p and d atomic orbitals to produce bonding and antibonding π orbitals molecular orbitals

The combination of p-orbital of one atom with the d-orbital of another atom is called p-d combination. This produces one bonding MO and one antibonding MO. As shown in figure 8.11.

In such a case, usually Py or Pz orbital of one atom overlap with d-orbital of the other atom to form a π bond. The lateral overlap of AOs produces π MOs.

8.9.3.4 Combination of d and d atomic orbitals

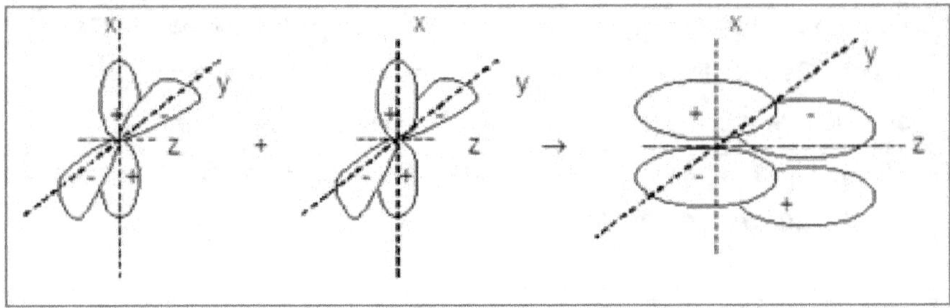

Figure 8.12: Formation of δ BMO by combination of $d_x{}^2{}_{-y}{}^2$ atomic orbitals

The combination of d-orbital of one atom with the d-orbital of the other atom is called d-d combination. This produces one bonding MO denoted as δ and one anti bonding MO denoted by δ*. The formation of δ MO takes place by the overlap of two d_{xy} or $d_x{}^2{}_{-y}{}^2$ AOs.

These δ MOs have two nodal planes along the molecular axis, as shown by dashed lines in figure 8.12 since the figure becomes complicated, formation of antibonding MO is shown here.

8.10 Rules for Linear Combination of Atomic Orbitals

1. If the two wave functions of the atomic orbitals have the same signs of the wave function, then it will result in the formation of a bonding MO.
2. If the two wave functions of the atomic orbitals have the different signs of the wave function, then it will result in the formation of a anti bonding MO.
3. The number of molecular orbitals formed will be equal to the number of atomic orbitals taking part in combination.
4. The atomic orbitals which are of lower energy or which do not have proper symmetry for combination will result in the formation of non-bonding MO.
5. If there are three atomic orbitals participating in the bond formation, they will result in the formation of one bonding, one anti-bonding and one non-bonding MO.
6. The AOs which form the MO should have comparable energies.

8.11 Non-bonding combination of orbitals

The orbitals which do not take part in bonding are called as non-bonding MOs. These orbitals of atoms are either very low in energy or they are not of proper symmetry hence they are not used for bonding. So they are called as non-bonding MOs. Figure 8.13 (i) shows the symmetries unsuitable for combination of s and p_x or p_y orbitals. Figure 8.13 (ii) shows the symmetries unsuitable for combination of p_x and p_y or p_z orbitals. Hence, they form non-bonding orbitals.

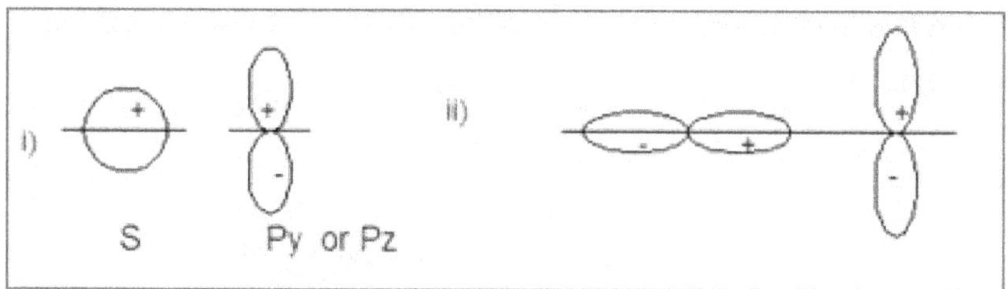

Figure 8.13: Formation of nonbonding molecular orbitals by combination of s and p atomic orbitals

8.12 MO Energy level diagram for homonuclear diatomic molecules of First Row Elements

First row of the periodic table contains only two elements hydrogen and helium. Both these elements have only 1s orbital in their atom. The combination of these two atoms of these elements gives a homonuclear diatomic molecule and He_2. When two 1s orbitals combine two molecular orbitals are formed- one bonding and one antibonding molecular orbitals. Combination of 1s and 1s gives σ molecular orbitals.

8.12.1 H_2^+ ion

It consists of two H atoms and one electron. Two 1s orbitals give two MOs – one bonding, that is σ and one anti bonding that is σ*. Formation of molecule can be explained in six steps as follows.

1) Electronic Configuration of H – $1s^1$

2) Molecular orbital energy level diagram: Since The bonding orbital is lower in energy, the electron occupies the bonding MO. Figure 8.14 shows the MO energy level diagram of H_2^+ molecular ion.

3) The molecular orbital electron configuration of H_2^+ ion is - $(1s)^1$.

4) The energy evolved during the formation of H_2^+ ion is calculated as

Energy evolved (E) = [No. of electrons in BMO x (-β) + No. of electrons in ABMO x (+β)]

= (1) x (-β) + (0) x (+β) = -β

The energy evolved -β is also called **stabilization energy**.

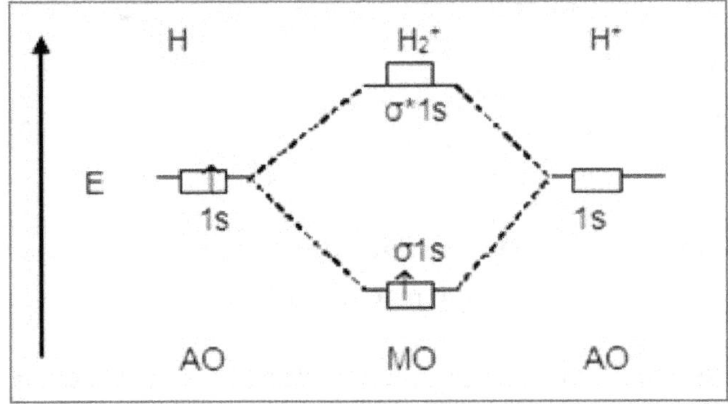

Figure 8.14: MO Energy level diagram of H_2^+ molecule

5) The number of bonds between the two atoms is called bond order. The bond order of this ion is calculated by the formula

Bond Order (B.O.) = ½ [No. of electrons in BMO – No. of electrons in ABMO]

= ½ (1- 0) =1/2

The molecular ion is expected to be somewhat stable. This species can be detected spectroscopically when hydrogen under reduced pressure is subjected to an electric discharge.

6) Since the H_2^+ ion has one unpaired electron, it is **paramagnetic**.

8.12.2 H_2 Molecule

H_2 Molecule consists of two H atoms and their two electrons. Two 1s orbitals give two MOs- one bonding that is σ and one antibonding that is σ*. Formation of molecule can be explained in six steps as follows.

1) Electronic Configuration of H – $1s^1$

2) Molecular orbital energy level diagram: Since The bonding orbital is lower in energy, the electron occupies the bonding MO. Figure 8.15 shows the MO energy level diagram of of H_2 Molecule.

3) The molecular orbital electron configuration of H_2 molecule is - $(1s)^2$.

4) The energy evolved during the formation of H_2 molecule is calculated as

Energy evolved (E) = [No. of electrons in BMO x $(-\beta)$ + No. of electrons in ABMO x $(+\beta)$]

$= (2) \times (-\beta) + (0) \times (+\beta) = -\beta$

The energy evolved -2β is also called **stabilization energy**.

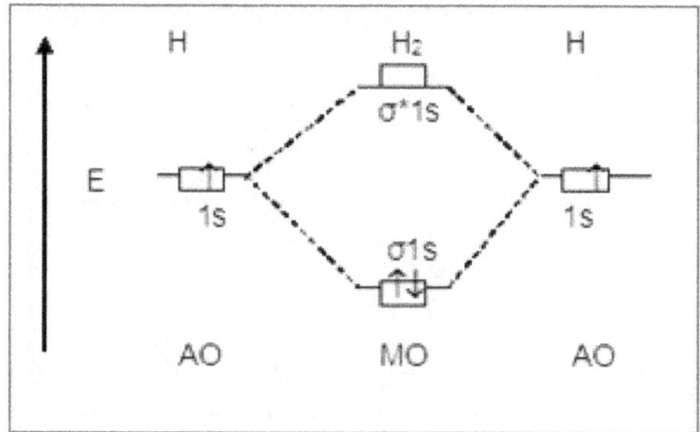

Figure 8.15: MO Energy level diagram of H_2 molecule

5) The number of bonds between the two atoms is called bond order. The bond order of this ion is calculated by the formula

Bond Order (B.O.) = ½ [No. of electrons in BMO – No. of electrons in ABMO]
 = ½ (2- 0) =1

The molecular is stable. This species can be detected spectroscopically when hydrogen under reduced pressure is subjected to an electric discharge.

6) Since the H_2 molecule has no any unpaired electron, it is **diamagnetic**.

8.12.3 He_2^+ ion

It consists of two He atoms and three electrons. One He atom gives $1s^2$ electrons and the other He atom gives $1s^1$ electron. Two 1s orbitals give two MOs – one bonding, that is σ and one anti bonding that is σ*. Formation of molecule can be explained in six steps as follows.

1) Electronic Configuration of He – $1s^2$

2) Molecular orbital energy level diagram: Since The bonding orbital is lower in energy, the electron occupies the bonding MO. Figure 8.16 shows the MO energy level diagram of of He_2^+ Molecule.

3) The molecular orbital electron configuration of He_2^+ molecule is - $(\sigma 1s)^2$, $(\sigma^*1s)^1$.

4) The energy evolved during the formation of He_2^+ molecule is calculated as

Energy evolved (E) = [No. of electrons in BMO x (-β) + No. of electrons in ABMO x (+β)]

= (2) x (-β) + (1) x (+β) = -β

The energy evolved -1β is also called **stabilization energy**.

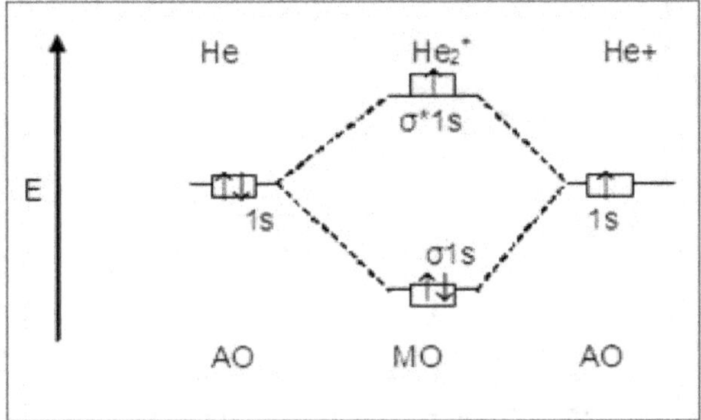

Figure 8.16: MO Energy level diagram of He_2^+ molecule

5) The number of bonds between the two atoms is called bond order. The bond order of this ion is calculated by the formula

Bond Order (B.O.) = ½ [No. of electrons in BMO – No. of electrons in ABMO]

= ½ (2- 1) =1/2

The molecular is stable. This species can be detected spectroscopically when hydrogen under reduced pressure is subjected to an electric discharge.

6) The molecular ion He_2^+ is expected to be somewhat stable. Since the He_2^+ ion has one unpaired electron, it is **paramagnetic**.

8.12.4 He₂ Molecule

It consists of two He atoms and four electrons. One He atom gives $1s^2$ electrons and the other He atom gives $1s^2$ electron. Two 1s orbitals give two MOs – one bonding, that is σ and one anti bonding that is σ*. Formation of molecule can be explained in six steps as follows.

1) Electronic Configuration of He – $1s^2$

2) Molecular orbital energy level diagram: Since The bonding orbital is lower in energy, the electron occupies the bonding MO. Figure 8.17 shows the MO energy level diagram of He_2 Molecule.

3) The molecular orbital electron configuration of He_2 molecule is - $(\sigma 1s)^2$, $(\sigma^* 1s)^2$.

4) The energy evolved during the formation of He_2 molecule is calculated as

Energy evolved (E) = [No. of electrons in BMO x (-β) + No. of electrons in ABMO x (+β)]

= (2) x (-β) + (2) x (+β) = 0

The energy evolved is zero, hence molecule is not **stable.**

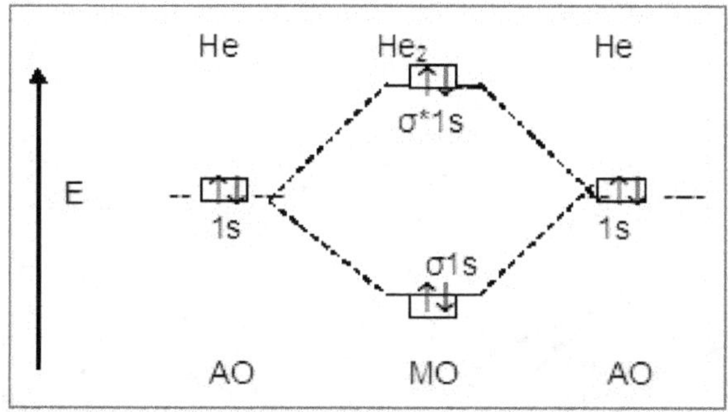

Figure 8.17: MO Energy level diagram of He_2 molecule

5) The number of bonds between the two atoms is called bond order. The bond order of this ion is calculated by the formula

Bond Order (B.O.) = ½ [No. of electrons in BMO – No. of electrons in ABMO]

= ½ (2- 2) = 0

The molecular is not stable.

6) The He_2 molecule is not stable and not in existence. Instead of formation of He_2 molecule, it remains in monoatomic state.

8.13 MO Energy level Diagram for Homonuclear Diatomic molecules of second Row Elements

Second row element contains 2s and 2p orbitals. The s orbital gives σ and σ* MOs. The overlap of Px and Px orbital gives σ px and σ*px MOs. The overlap of py and py orbital gives πpy and π*py MOs. The overlap of pz and pz orbitals gives πpz and π*pz MOs. The πpy and πpz Mos and similarly the π*py and π*pz MOs have equivalent energies hence they are said to be **degenerate**. The magnitude of the overlap decreases in the order s-s = pσ – pσ > pπ – pπ . Hence the value of Δ or β also decreases in the same manner. The energy sequence of the MOs is

σ1s < σ*1s < σ2px < π2py = π2pz < π*2py = π*2pz < σ*2px.

The diagram 8.18 and the sequence of energy level assumes that s atomic orbital overlap with only s atomic orbital, p atomic orbital overlap with only p atomic orbital i.e. there is no interaction between s and p orbitals of a given atom.

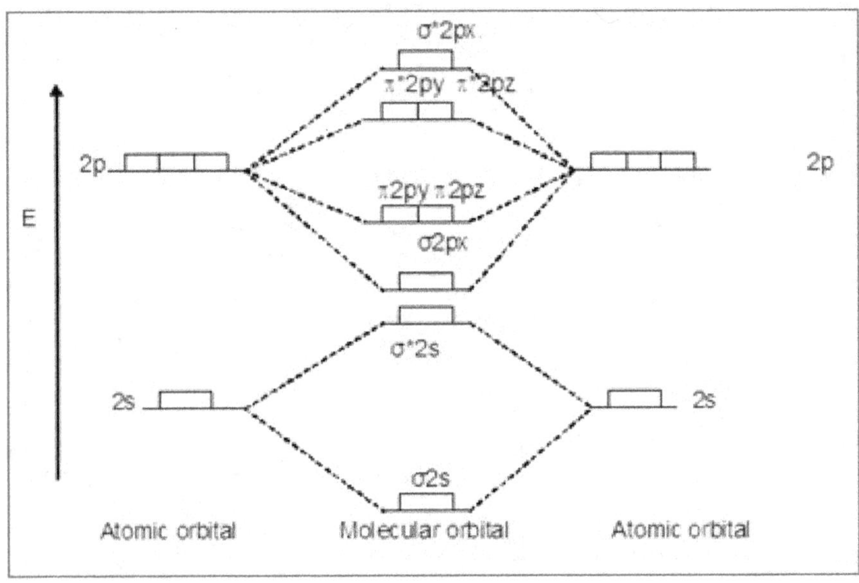

Figure 8.18: MO Energy level diagram in which there is no interaction between s and p orbitals

In practice, such an interaction does take place and the sequence of energy levels is changed. In Li_2, Be_2, B_2, C_2 and N_2 the energy difference between 2s and 2p atomic orbitals is not large and they are likely to ineract when permitted by symmetry. Consequently, s and px atomic orbitals interact with one another resulting in the repulsion between pairs of orbitals of the same type, i.e. σ2s and σ2px and two σ* orbitals, i.e. σ*2s and σ*2px.The new sequence of MOs for Li_2, Be_2, B_2, C_2 and N_2 thus becomes

σ1s < σ*1s < σ2s < σ*2s < π2py =π2pz < σ2px < π*2py = π*2pz < σ*2px.

After nitrogen the energy difference between S and p atomic orbitals becomes sufficiently large and such effect may be practically neglected. The occupancy of available homonuclear orbitals in energy order is easily understood from the energy level diagram Figure 8.19.

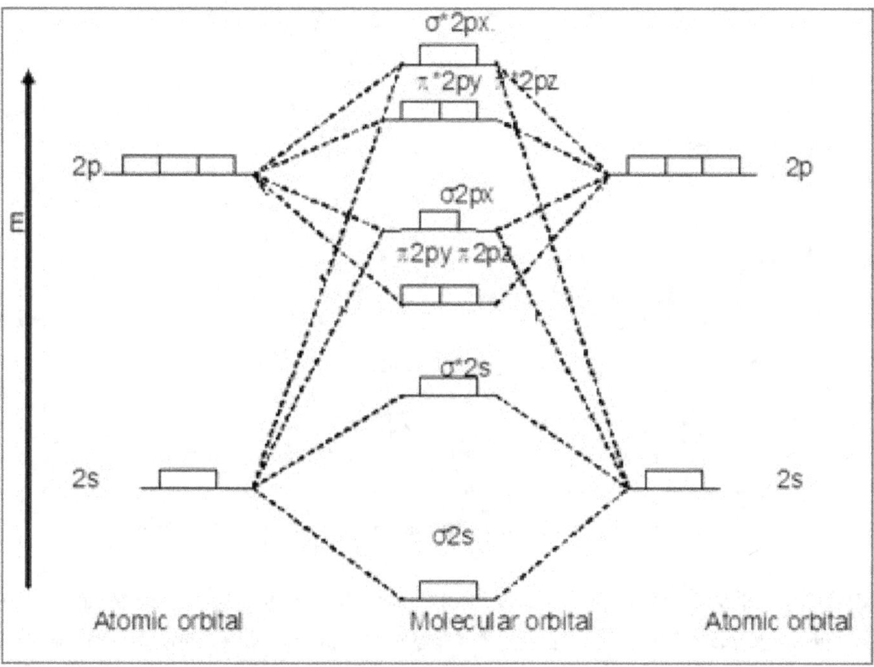

Figure 8.19: MO Energy level diagram in which there is interaction between s and p orbitals

8.13.1 Li$_2$ Molecule

This molecule is formed by the combination of two lithium atoms. Formation of molecule can be explained in six steps as follows.

1) Each lithium atom has electron configuration 1s^2, 2s^1. The 1s orbital is lower in energy so it does not take part in bonding. Thus, 1s orbital remain as a non-bonding orbital. Only the 2s orbital with its one electron takes part in bonding. Since there are two atomic orbitals, they will form two MOs. σ and σ*. There are two electrons which enter the bonding MO i.e. σ.

2) MO Energy level diagram of Li$_2$ Molecule is shown in figure 8.20.

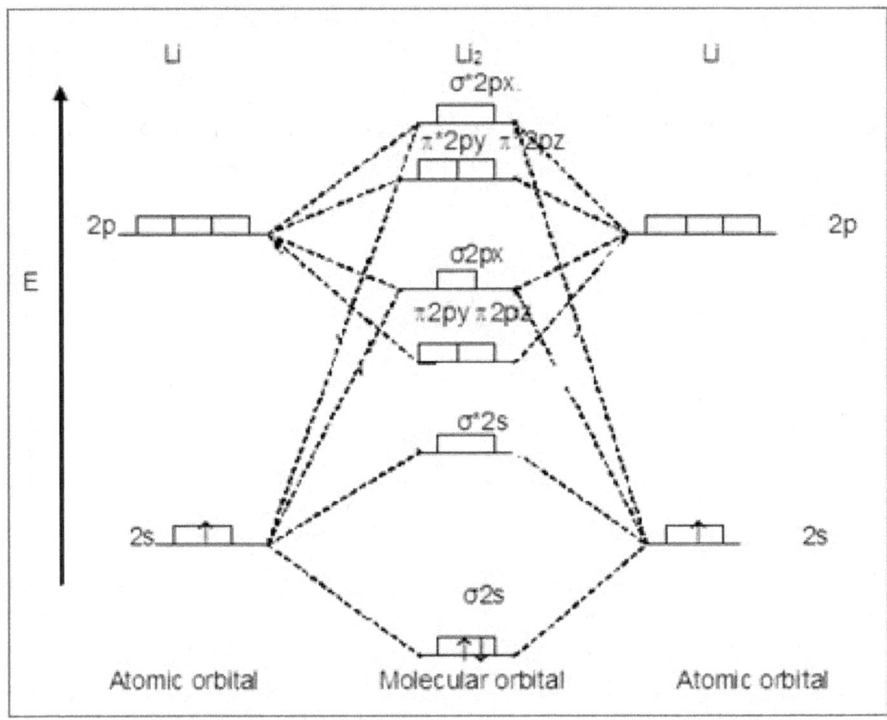

Figure 8.20: MO Energy level diagram of Li$_2$ molecule

3) MO electron configuration of Li$_2$ Molecule: The presence of non-bonding 1s^2 electron is shown by capital letter K because these two electrons are present in the first shell i.e. K shell. There are two Li atoms taking part in bonding so the letter K is repeated. The remaining two electrons of the Li$_2$ Molecule go to the BMO. The MO electron configuration of Li$_2$ Molecule is written as [KK (σ2s)^2].

4) The energy evolved during the formation of molecule is calculated as

Energy evolved (E) = [No. of electrons in BMO x (-β) + No. of electrons in ABMO x (+β)]

= (2) x (-β) + (0) x (+β) = -2 β

5) The number of bonds between the two atoms is called bond order. The bond order of this molecule is calculated by the formula

Bond Order = ½ [No. of electrons in BMO – No. of electrons in ABMO]

$$= ½ (2- 0) = 1$$

The bond order is one. The bond energy is 25 Kcal/mole. Li_2 Molecule exist in vapour state.

6) Since all the electrons are paired, the molecule is diamagnetic. Li_2 Molecule is compared with H_2 Molecule, both these molecules are diamagnetic. They have bond order one.

H_2 Molecule	Li_2 Molecule
1) Bond length = 0.74 A^0	1) Bond length = 2.67 A^0
2) Bond energy = 103 Kcal	2)Bond energy = 25 Kcal

Bond energy of Li_2 Molecule is less than H_2 molecule because 2s and 2p orbitals of Li atom are much larger and more diffuse than the 1s orbital of hydrogen. They tend to overlap less effectively and at a greater internuclear distance than in case of 1s orbital of H.

The 1s electron of Li cause a repulsion between the atoms which loosens closer approach of the atoms. Due to above two reasons, bond length in Li_2 Molecule is more than that in H_2 Molecule and bond energy in Li_2 Molecule is less than that in H_2 Molecule.

8.13.2 Be$_2$ Molecule

Be_2 Molecule is formed by the combination of two beryllium atoms. Formation of molecule can be explained in six steps as follows.

1) The electronic configuration of beryllium atom is $1s^2, 2s^2$. The 1s orbital is lower in energy so it does not take part in bonding. Thus 1s orbital remain as a non-bonding orbital. Only the 2s orbital with its two electron takes part in bonding. Since there are two atomic orbitals, they will form two MOs. σ and σ^*.

The first two electrons enter the BMO and the next two electrons enter the ABMO.

2) MO Energy level diagram of Be_2 Molecule:

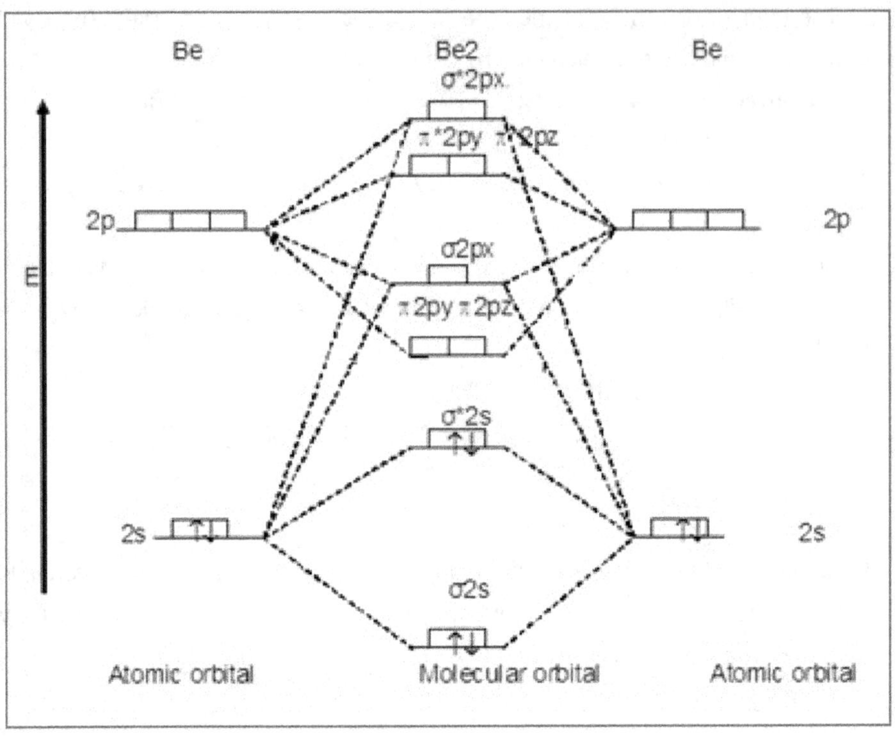

Figure 8.21: MO Energy level diagram of Be_2 molecule

3) MO electron configuration of Be_2 Molecule: The presence of non-bonding $1s^2$ electron is shown by capital letter K because these two electrons are present in the first shell i.e. K shell. There are two Be atoms taking part in bonding so the letter K is repeated. The two electrons of the Be_2 Molecule go to the BMO and two electrons in the ABMO. Fig. 1.19 shows the MO Energy level diagram of Be_2 Molecule. The MO electron configuration of Be_2 Molecule is written as [KK $(σ2s)^2$, $(σ*2s)^2$].

4) The energy evolved during the formation of molecule is calculated as

Energy evolved (E) = [No. of electrons in BMO x (-β) + No. of electrons in ABMO x (+β)]

= (2) x (-β) + (2) x (+β) = 0

5) The number of bonds between the two atoms is called bond order. The bond order of this molecule is calculated by the formula

Bond Order = ½ [No. of electrons in BMO – No. of electrons in ABMO]

$$= ½ (2-2) = 0$$

The bond order is zero. The bond energy is zero. Be_2 Molecule is not in existence.

6) The Be_2 molecule is not stable and not in existence. Instead of formation of Be_2 molecule, it remains in monoatomic state.

8.13.3 B_2 Molecule

This molecule is formed by the combination of two Boron atoms. Formation of molecule can be explained in six steps as follows.

1) Electronic configuration of each Boron atom is $1s^2$, $2s^2$, $2p^1$. The 1s orbital is lower in energy so it does not take part in bonding. Thus 1s orbital remain as a non-bonding orbital. Only two 2s orbital and six 2p orbitals of two boron atoms i.e. total eight orbitals form total eight MOs. Here 2s and 2p orbitals of boron atom are close in energy so they interact and the sequence of energy levels of MOs is according to figure 8.19.

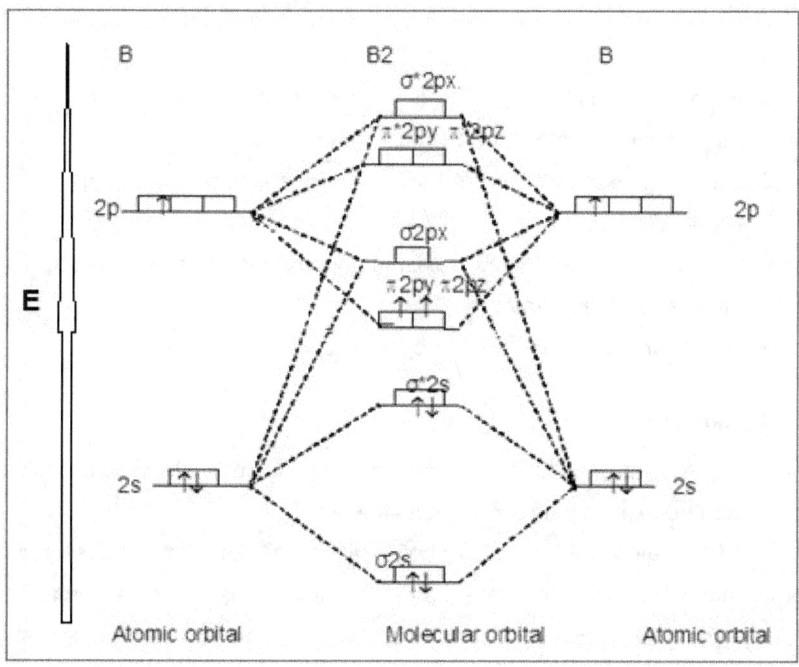

2) MO Energy level diagram of B_2 Molecule: Figure 8.22 shows the MO Energy level diagram of B_2 Molecule.

3) MO electron configuration of B_2 Molecule: The presence of non-bonding $1s^2$ electron is shown by capital letter K because these two electrons are present in the first shell i.e. K shell. There are two B atoms taking part in bonding so the letter K is repeated. The remaining six electrons of the B_2 Molecular orbital following Aufbau principle and Hund's rule of maximum multiplicity. First two electrons go to σ2s BMO, the next two go to the σ*2s BMO. The remaining two electrons occupy the π2py and π2pz orbitals with parallel spins. These two orbitals are degenerate. The MO electron configuration of B_2 Molecule is written as

$$[KK \ (σ2s)^2, \ (σ^*2s)^2, \ (π2py)^1,(π2pz)^1].$$

The stabilization energy is found out as follows.

4) The energy evolved during the formation of molecule is calculated as

Energy evolved (E) = [No. of electrons in BMO x (-β) + No. of electrons in ABMO x (+β)]

= (4) x (-β) + (2) x (+β)   = -2 β

5) The number of bonds between the two atoms is called bond order. The bond order of this molecule is calculated by the formula

Bond Order = ½ [No. of electrons in BMO – No. of electrons in ABMO]

= ½ (4-2) = 1

The bond order is one. B_2 Molecule exist in vapour state. It has bond length 1.59 A^0 and bond energy 69 Kcal/mole.

6) Since two electrons are unpaired, the molecule is paramagnetic.

8.13.4 C_2 Molecule

C_2 Molecule is formed by the combination of two carbon atoms. Formation of molecule can be explained in six steps as follows.

1) Each carbon atom has electron configuration $1s^2$, $2s^2$, $2p^2$. The 1s orbital is lower in energy so it does not take part in bonding. Thus 1s orbital remain as a non-bonding orbital. Only two 2s orbital and six 2p orbitals of two carbon atoms i.e. total eight orbitals form total eight MOs. Here 2s and 2p orbitals of carbon

atom are close in energy so they interact and the sequence of energy levels of MOs is according to Figure 8.19 in C_2 Molecule.

2) MO Energy level diagram of C_2 Molecule: Figure 8.23 shows the MO Energy level diagram of C_2 Molecule.

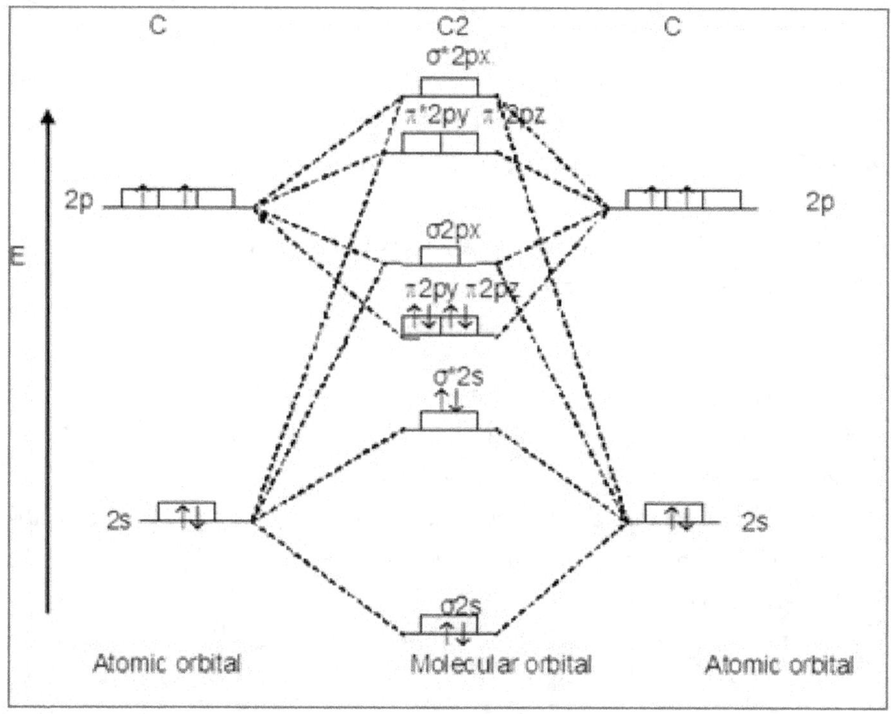

Figure 8.23: MO Energy level diagram of C_2 molecule

3) MO electron configuration of C_2 Molecule: The presence of non-bonding $1s^2$ electron is shown by capital letter K because these two electrons are present in the first shell i.e. K shell. There are two C atoms taking part in bonding so the letter K is repeated. The remaining eight electrons of the C_2 Molecular orbital following Aufbau principle and Hund's rule of maximum multiplicity. First two electrons go to σ2s BMO, the next two go to the σ*2s BMO. The remaining four electrons occupy the π2py and π2pz orbitals. These two orbitals are degenerate. Figure 8.23 shows the MO Energy level diagram of C_2 Molecule. The MO

125

electron configuration of C_2 Molecule is written as [KK $(\sigma 2s)^2$, $(\sigma^* 2s)^2$, $(\pi 2py)^2$, $(\pi 2pz)^2$]. The stabilization energy is found out as follows.

4) The energy evolved during the formation of molecule is calculated as

Stabilization Energy = [No. of electrons in BMO x $(-\beta)$ + No. of electrons in ABMO x $(+\beta)$]

= (6) x $(-\beta)$ + (2) x $(+\beta)$ = -4 β

5) The number of bonds between the two atoms is called bond order. The bond order of this molecule is calculated by the formula

Bond Order = ½ [No. of electrons in BMO – No. of electrons in ABMO]

$$= \frac{1}{2}(6\text{-}2) = 2$$

The bond order is two. C_2 Molecule exist in vapour state. It has bond length 1.31 A^0 and bond energy 150 Kcal/mole.

6) Since all electrons are paired, the molecule is diamagnetic.

8.13.5 N_2 Molecule

This molecule is formed by the combination of two nitrogen atoms. Formation of molecule can be explained in six steps as follows.

1) Each nitrogen atom has electron configuration $1s^2$, $2s^2$, $2p^3$. The 1s orbital is lower in energy so it does not take part in bonding. Thus, 1s orbital remain as a non-bonding orbital.

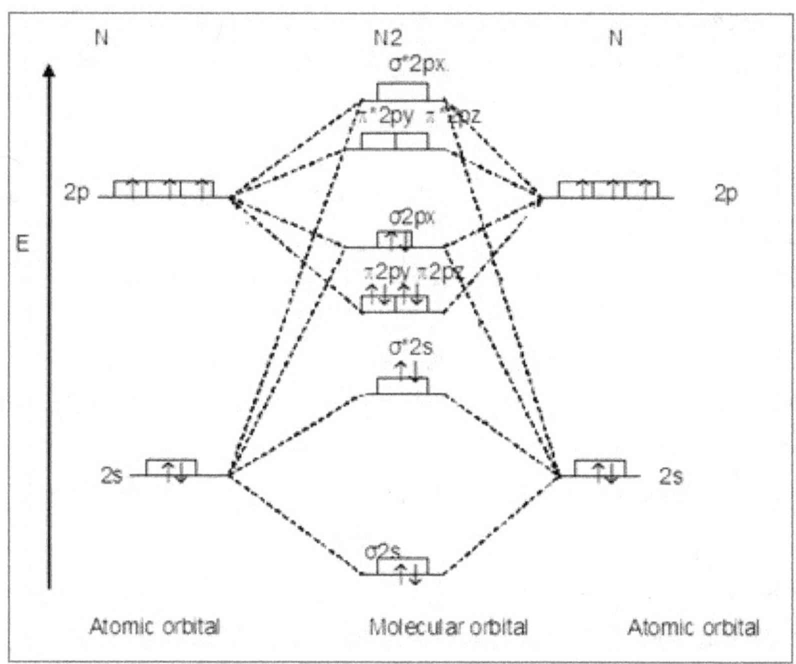

Figure 8.24: MO Energy level diagram of N$_2$ molecule

Only two 2s orbital and six 2p orbitals of two nitrogen atoms i.e. total eight orbitals form total eight MOs. Here 2s and 2p orbitals of nitrogen atom are close in energy so they interact and the sequence of energy levels of MOs is according to figure 8.19 in N$_2$ Molecule.

2) MO Energy level diagram of N$_2$ Molecule: Figure 8.24 shows the MO Energy level diagram of N$_2$ Molecule.

3) MO electron configuration of N$_2$ Molecule: The presence of non-bonding 1s^2 electron is shown by capital letter K because these two electrons are present in the first shell i.e.K shell. There are two N atoms taking part in bonding so the letter K is repeated. The remaining ten electrons of the N$_2$ Molecular orbital following Aufbau principle and Hund's rule of maximum multiplicity. First two electrons go to σ2s BMO, the next two go to the σ*2s ABMO, four electrons go to the π2py and π2pz orbitals and the remaining two occupy the σ2px.

The MO electron configuration of N$_2$ Molecule is written as [KK (σ2s)^2, (σ*2s)^2, (π2py)^2, (π2pz)^2 (σ2px)^2]. The stabilization energy is found out as follows.

4) The energy evolved during the formation of molecule is calculated as

Stabilisation Energy = [No. of electrons in BMO $_x$ $(-\beta)$ + No. of electrons in ABMO x $(+\beta)$]

= (8) x $(-\beta)$ + (2) x $(+\beta)$ = $- 6\beta$

5) The number of bonds between the two atoms is called bond order. The bond order of this molecule is calculated by the formula

Bond Order = ½ [No. of electrons in BMO – No. of electrons in ABMO]

$$= ½ (8 - 2) = 3$$

The bond order is three. N_2 Molecule contains one σ and two π bonds. It has bond length 1.10 A^0 and bond energy 226 Kcal/mole. N_2 Molecule is highly stable and chemically inert.

6) Since all electrons in N_2 Molecule are paired, the molecule is diamagnetic.

8.13.6 O_2 Molecule

This molecule is formed by the combination of two oxygen atoms. Formation of molecule can be explained in six steps as follows.

1) Each oxygen atom has electron configuration $1s^2$, $2s^2$, $2p^4$.The1s orbital is lower in energy so it does not take part in bonding. Thus 1s orbital remain as a non-bonding orbital. Only two 2s orbital and six 2p orbitals of two oxygen atoms i.e. total eight orbitals form total eight MOs. Here 2s and 2p orbitals of oxygen atom are well separated in energy so they do not interact and the sequence of energy levels of MOs in O_2 molecule is according to Figure 8.18.

2) MO Energy level diagram of N_2 Molecule: The MO energy level diagram for oxygen molecule is shown in figure 8.25.

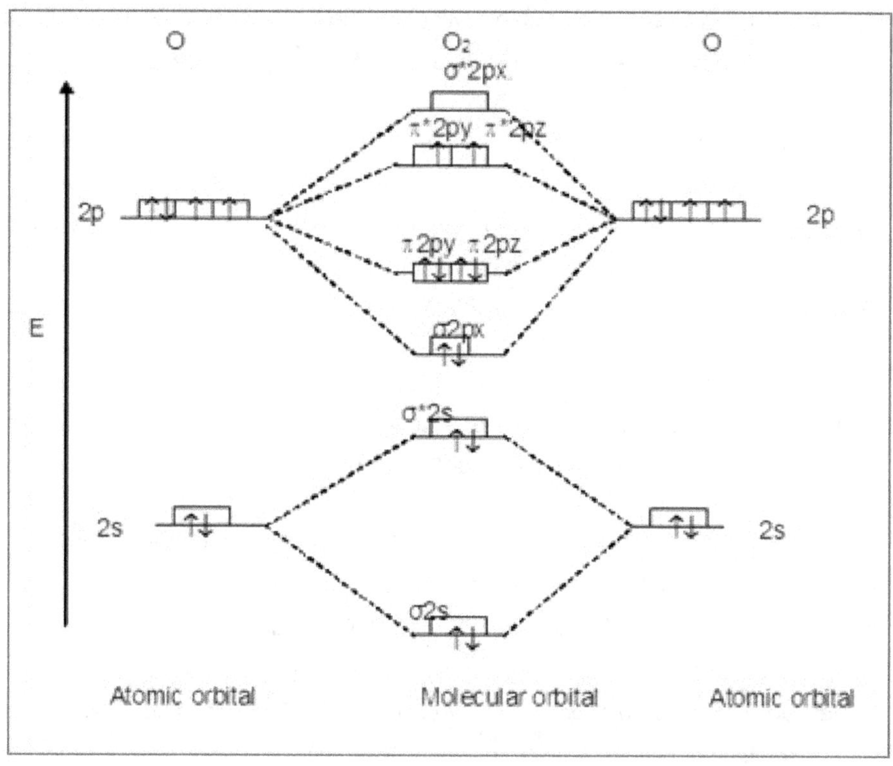

Figure 8.25: MO Energy level diagram of O$_2$ molecule

3) MO electron configuration of O$_2$ Molecule: The presence of non-bonding 1s^2 electron is shown by capital letter K because these two electrons are present in the first shell i.e. K shell. There are two O atoms taking part in bonding so the letter K is repeated. The remaining twelve electrons of the O$_2$ Molecular orbital following Aufbau principle and Hund's rule of maximum multiplicity. First two electrons go to σ2s BMO, the next two go to the σ*2s ABMO, two electrons occupy the σ2px and the four electrons go to the π2py and π2pz orbitals and remaining two electrons go to the π*2py and π*2pz orbitals.

The MO electron configuration of O$_2$ Molecule is written as [KK(σ2s)^2, (σ*2s)^2, (σ2px)^2, (π2py)^2, (π2pz)^2, (π*2py)^1, (π*2pz)^1]. The stabilization energy is found out as follows.

4) The energy evolved during the formation of molecule is calculated as

Stabilization Energy = [No. of electrons in BMO $\times$ (-β) + No. of electrons in ABMO x (+β)]

= (8) x (-β) + (4) x (+β) = - 4 β

5) The number of bonds between the two atoms is called bond order. The bond order of this molecule is calculated by the formula

Bond Order = ½ [No. of electrons in BMO – No. of electrons in ABMO]

$$= ½ (8\text{-}4) = 2$$

There is double bond in O_2 Molecule. It contains one σ and one π bond. It has bond length 1.21 A^0 and bond energy 118 Kcal/mole.

6) Magnetic property of O_2 Molecule: In O_2 Molecule two unpaired electrons with parallel spins in the degenerate antibonding π MOs are shown in fig.1.23 .This distribution of electrons in the antibonding π MOs is according to Hund's rule. Oxygen molecule shows paramagnetic properties. MO theory gives a very simple explanation for the presence of two unpaired electrons and hence the paramagnetism of oxygen molecule.

It is very difficult to explain the paramagnetism of oxygen molecule with the help of VBT. The VBT assumes the sharing of electrons between the two oxygen atoms for the completion of octet configuration of each oxygen atom in the oxygen molecule. According to VBT oxygen molecule should be diamagnetic but in practice, it is paramagnetic. MO theory explains the paramagnetic of oxygen molecule.

Effect of number of electrons in the antibonding MOs on bond lengths in diatomic species of oxygen:

O_2^- ion:

O_2^- superoxide ion, is an example of molecular species. It has one electron more than the electrons of the O_2 molecule. Thus it has 17 electrons. Its MO representation is:

O_2^- = [KK(σ2s)^2, (σ*2s)^2 , (σ2px)^2 (π2py)^2,(π2pz)^2 (π*2py)^2,(π*2pz)^1]

It has one unpaired electron. The Bond order (BO) = ½(8- 5) = 1.5

Thus there is one σ bond and one three electron bond.

O_2^{-2} ion: In a peroxide ion ($O_2^{-2)}$ there are two electrons more than the electrons in oxygen molecule. Thus it has 18 electrons and no unpaired electrons. Its MO representation is:

O_2^{-2} =[KK(σ2s)^2, (σ*2s)^2, (σ2px)^2 (π2py)^2, (π2pz)^2 (π*2py)^2, (π*2pz)^2]

The Bond order (BO) = ½ (8-6) = 1 Thus there is one σ bond.

Ion	Total number of electrons	Bond Order	Magnetic Property
O_2^+	15	2.5	Paramagnetic
O_2	16	2.0	Paramagnetic
O_2^-	17	1.5	Paramagnetic
O_2^{-2}	18	1.0	Dimagnetic

O_2^+ ion: The O_2^+ positive ion is formed by losing one electron from the antibonding MO of the oxygen molecule. The bond order of O_2 is 2 while that of O_2^+ ion is 2.5 this result into the decrease of bond distance.

8.13.7 F_2 molecule

This molecule is formed by the combination of two fluorine atoms. Formation of molecule can be explained in six steps as follows.

1) Each fluorine atom has electron configuration 1s^2, 2s^2, 2p^5.The1s orbital is lower in energy so it does not take part in bonding. Thus 1s orbital remain as a non-bonding orbital. Only two 2s orbital and six 2p orbitals of two oxygen atoms i.e. total eight orbitals form total eight MOs. Here 2s and 2p orbitals of fluorine atom are well separated in energy so they do not interact and the sequence of energy levels of MOs in F_2 molecule is according to Figure 8.18

2) 2) MO Energy level diagram of N_2 Molecule: The MO energy level diagram for oxygen molecule is shown in figure 8.26.

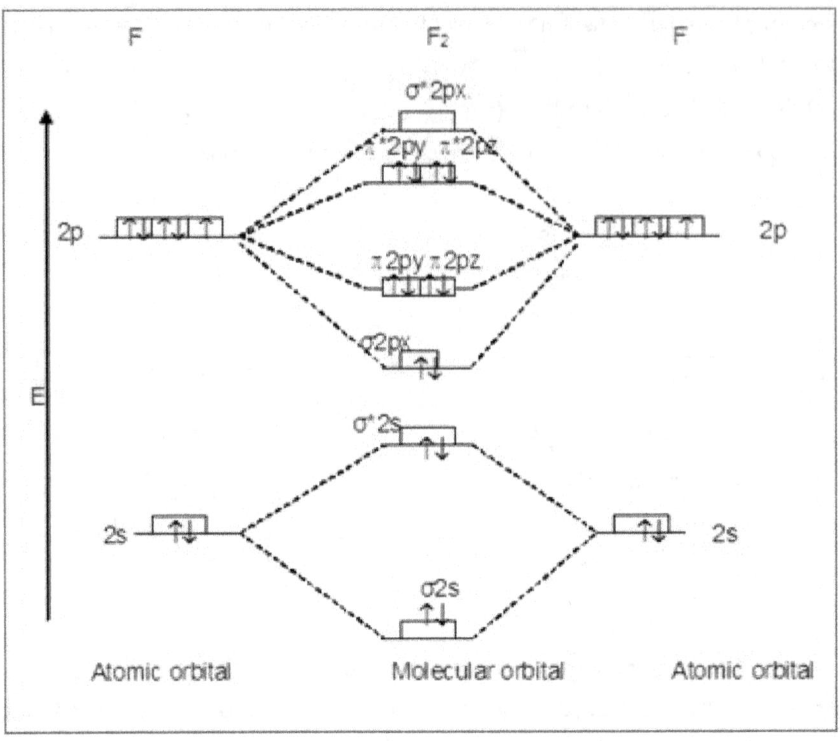

Figure 8.26: MO Energy level diagram of F_2 molecule

3) MO electron configuration of F_2 Molecule: The presence of non-bonding $1s^2$ electron is shown by capital letter K because these two electrons are present in the first shell i.e. K shell. There are two F atoms taking part in bonding so the letter K is repeated. The remaining fourteen electrons of the O_2 Molecular orbital following Aufbau principle and Hund's rule of maximum multiplicity. First two electrons go to σ2s BMO, the next two go to the σ*2s ABMO, two electrons occupy the σ2px four electrons go to the π2py and π2pz orbitals and the remaining four electrons go to the π*2py and π*2pz orbitals

The MO electron configuration of F_2 Molecule is written as [KK$(\sigma 2s)^2$, $(\sigma^*2s)^2$, $(\sigma 2px)^2$, $(\pi 2py)^2$, $(\pi 2pz)^2$, $(\pi^*2py)^2$, $(\pi^*2pz)^2$]. The stabilization energy is found out as follows.

4) The energy evolved during the formation of molecule is calculated as
Stabilization Energy = [No. of electrons in BMO $\times$ $(-\beta)$ + No. of electrons in ABMO x $(+\beta)$]
= (8) x $(-\beta)$ + (6) x $(+\beta)$ = - 2 β

5) The number of bonds between the two atoms is called bond order. The bond order of this molecule is calculated by the formula
Bond Order = ½ [No. of electrons in BMO – No. of electrons in ABMO]
= ½ (8-6) = 1
There is single bond in F_2 Molecule. It contains one σ bond. It has bond length 1.44 A^0 and bond energy 38 Kcal/mole. The molecule is stable.

6) Since all electrons in N_2 Molecule are paired, the molecule is diamagnetic.

8.13.8 Ne_2 Molecule

In this molecule all the orbitals are filled by electrons, so bond order is zero. Stabilization energy is also zero. Ne_2 Molecule is not stable so it does not exist. (Explanation is similar to that of He_2 Molecule)

8.14 MO Energy level Diagram for Heteronuclear Diatomic molecules

8.14.1 Carbon monoxide Molecule (CO)
Carbon monoxide is a heteronuclear diatomic molecule. It is formed by the combination of carbon atom and oxygen atom. Formation of molecule can be explained in six steps as follows.

1) Oxygen is more electronegative than carbon. The electron configuration of carbon is $1s^2$, $2s^2$, $2p^2$ and that of oxygen is $1s^2$, $2s^2$, $2p^4$. The inner 1s electron of C and O don't take part in bonding.

2) The Carbon monoxide Molecule is isoelectronic with N_2 molecule. Both of them have ten electrons. The MO energy level diagram of N_2 molecule is similar

to that of CO molecule. Except that the energy level of oxygen are lower than that of carbon atom. Figure 8.27 shows the energy level diagram of CO molecule.

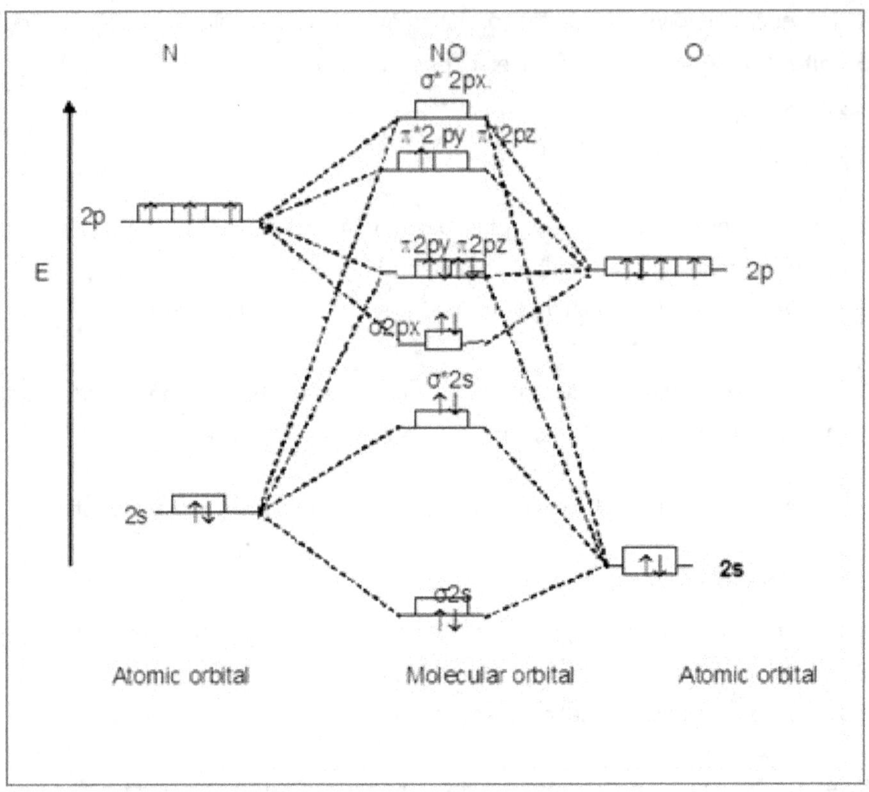

Figure 8.27: MO Energy level diagram of CO molecule

3) MO electron configuration of CO Molecule: Since oxygen is more electronegative than carbon, its energy level is lower than those of carbon. The oxygen orbital contributes more to the antibonding MO. The eight electrons in the bonding MO try to neutralize the greater nuclear charge on the oxygen core. Hence the polarity of CO is low. The MO electron configuration of CO molecule is KK $(\sigma 2s)^2$, $(\sigma^* 2s)^2$,$(\pi 2py)^2$,$(\pi 2pz)^2$ $(\sigma 2px)^2$]

4) The energy evolved during the formation of molecule is calculated as

Stabilization Energy = No. of electrons in BMO x (-β) + No.of electrons in ABMO x (+β)] = (8) x (-β) + (2) x (+β) = - 6 β

5) The number of bonds between the two atoms is called bond order. The bond order of this molecule is calculated by the formula

Bond order = ½ (8-2) = 3

The CO molecule contains a triple bond. There is one σ and two π bonds. The bond length in CO molecule is 1.128 A⁰ and bond energy 225 Kcal/mole.

6) Since all electrons in CO Molecule unpaired electrons present, the molecule is paramagnetic.

8.14.2 Nitric Oxide (NO) Molecule

Nitric oxide is a heteronuclear diatomic molecule. It is formed by the combination of nitrogen atom and oxygen atom. Here oxygen is more electronegative than nitrogen. Formation of molecule can be explained in six steps as follows.

1) The electron configuration of nitrogen is $1s^2$, $2s^2$, $2p^3$ and that of oxygen is is $1s^2$, $2s^2$, $2p^4$. The inner 1s electron of N and O do not take part in bonding. The MO electron configuration of NO Molecule can be qualitatively obtained either by removing one electron from the configuration of O_2 molecule or by adding one electron to the configuration of N_2 molecule.

2) MO energy level diagram of NO molecule: MO energy level diagram of NO molecule is shown in figure 8.28. Since oxygen is more electronegative than nitrogen, its energy level are lower than those of carbon.

3) MO electron configuration of CO Molecule: The oxygen orbital contributes more to the antibonding MO. The eight electrons in the bonding MO try to neutralize the greater nuclear charge on the oxygen core. Hence the polarity of NO is low. The MO electron configuration of NO molecule is [KK (σ2s)2, (σ*2s)2 , (σ2px)² (π2py)²,(π2pz)²(π*2py)¹]

4) The energy evolved during the formation of molecule is calculated as

Stabilization Energy = No. of electrons in BMO x (-β) + No.of electrons in ABMO x (+β)]

= (8) x (-β) + (3) x (+β) = - 5 β

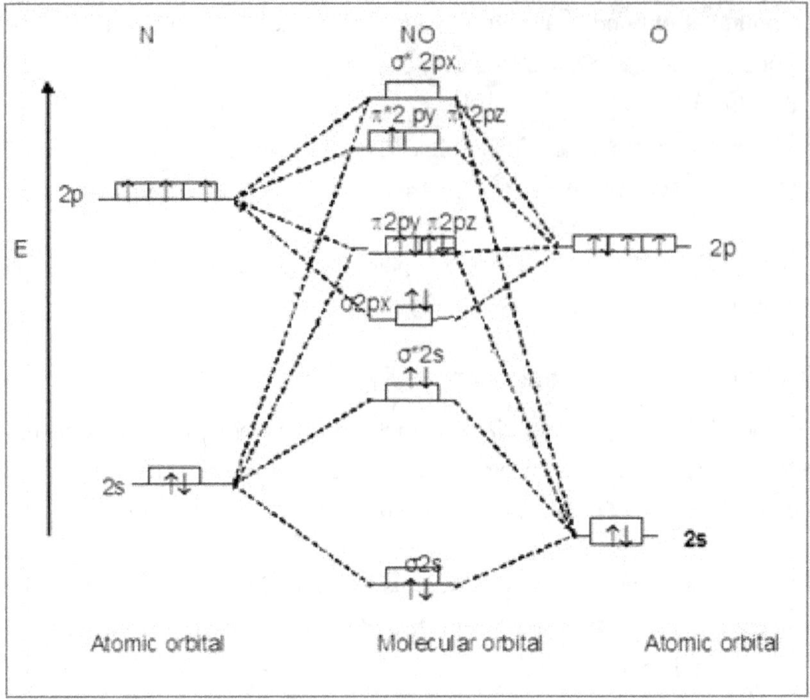

Figure 8.28: MO Energy level diagram of NO molecule

5) The number of bonds between the two atoms is called bond order. The bond order of this molecule is calculated by the formula

Bond order = ½ (8-3) = 2.5

The bond length in NO molecule is 1.15 A^0 and bond energy 162 Kcal/mole. which is considerably less than that of O_2 or N_2 molecule.

6) There is one unpaired electron in the (π^*) orbital so the molecule is paramagnetic.

Nitrosyl Ion (NO⁺)

In the process of ionization, NO loses one electron and forms NO^+ ion. The electron is removed from the antibonding (π*2py) orbital. The Mo electron configuration of NO$^+$ ion is

$$[K\ K, (\sigma 2s)2, (\sigma^*2s)2, (\sigma 2px)^2, (\pi 2py)^2, (\pi 2pz)^2]$$

The bond order of NO$^+$ ion is   Bond order = ½ (8-2) = 3

Thus the bond in NO$^+$ ion stronger and shorter than that in NO. the NO$^+$ forms stable compound like NO, HSO_4 (NO$^+$. HSO4$^-$)

8.14.3 Hydrogen chloride (HCl) Molecule

It is a heteronuclear diatomic molecule in which chlorine atom is much more electronegative than hydrogen. Formation of molecule can be explained in six steps as follows.

1) The electron configuration of H is $1s^1$ and that of Cl is $1s^2, 2s^2, 2p^6, 3s^2, 3p^5$. The atomic orbitals of more electronegative element contribute more to the formation of bonding MO and less to the antibonding MO. Similarly, the atomic orbital of less electronegative element contributes more to the formation of antibonding MO and less to the bonding MO. That is the electron in the MO spent more time round one atom than the other. This causes charge separation and, on the atoms, and develops a dipole, thus the covalent bond in HCl molecule has partial ionic character.

2) MO energy level diagram of HCl molecule: Let us consider the formation of MO in HCl molecule. It is shown that the filled 1s, 2s, 2p and 3s orbitals of chlorine atom are lower in energy and hence can not participate in bonding. Only the 3p orbitals of chlorine atom of suitable energy and can combine with the 1s orbital of hydrogen. If we assume H-Cl axis as the x-axis, then only the 3Px orbital of chlorine atom is of correct symmetry pointing along H-Cl axis. Thus out of the three 3Px orbitals only 3Px orbital of chlorine will be the most suitable one for bonding because it matches in symmetry and energy with the 1s orbital of hydrogen.

The other two 3p orbitals viz. 3py and 3pz being perpendicular to the bond axis are not of correct symmetry and hence remain nonbonding. The overlapping of 1s orbital of hydrogen and 3px orbital of chlorine gives rise to σ a bonding MO and σ^* MO. Figure 8.29 shows the MO energy level diagram of HCl molecule.

3) MO electronic configuration of HCl molecule: While writing the electron configuration of HCl molecule, for H atom there are no electrons to be written as k shell. However, for Cl atom, for $1s^2$ electrons we write k and for $2s^2$ and $2p^6$ electrons we write L. Neglecting the $3s^2$, $3p_y^2$ and $3p_z^2$ electrons of chlorine atom, the MO electron configuration of HCL molecule is written as [K L $(\sigma sp)^2$]. The two electron occupy the bonding MO.

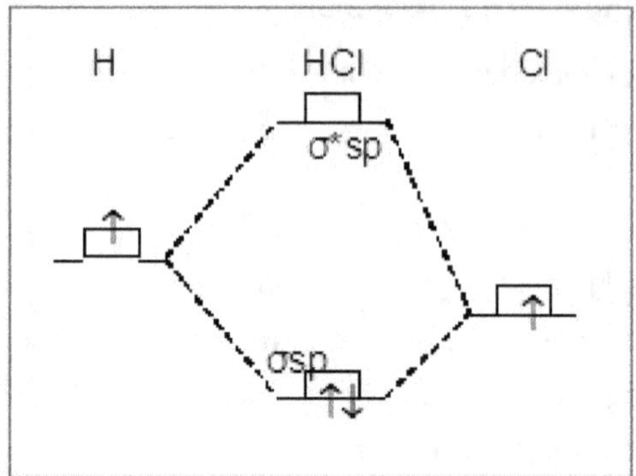

Figure 8.29: MO Energy level diagram of HCl molecule

4) The energy evolved during the formation of HCl molecule is calculated as
Stabilization Energy = No. of electrons in BMO x (-β) + No.of electrons in ABMO x (+β)]
= (2) x (-β) + (0) x (+β) = - 2 β

5) The number of bonds between the two atoms is called bond order. The bond order of this molecule is calculated by the formula
Bond order = ½ (2-0) = 1.0

The bond order is one. The bonding MO is closer to $3p_x$ orbital of chlorine atom hence it has more character of 3px orbital. the antibonding MO is closer to 1s orbital of hydrogen atom so it has more character of 1s orbital. H-Cl molecule is a polar and H-Cl bond is a polar covalent bond. The bond length in HCl molecule is $1.27A^0$ and bond energy is 103 kcal/ mole.

 6) The HCl molecule is diamagnetic.

8.15 Molecular Orbitals in Heteronuclear Triatomic Molecules

The molecules formed by three atoms of two different elements are called heteronuclear triatomic molecules. E.g. CO_2, NO_2, NO_2^- (nitrite molecule). These molecules may contain only sigma bond or both sigma and pi bonds.

8.15.1 Molecular orbital diagram for carbon dioxide (CO_2) molecule

It is linear triatomic molecule. It is represented as

$$O \overset{\sigma}{\underset{\pi}{=}} C \overset{\sigma}{\underset{\pi}{=}} O$$

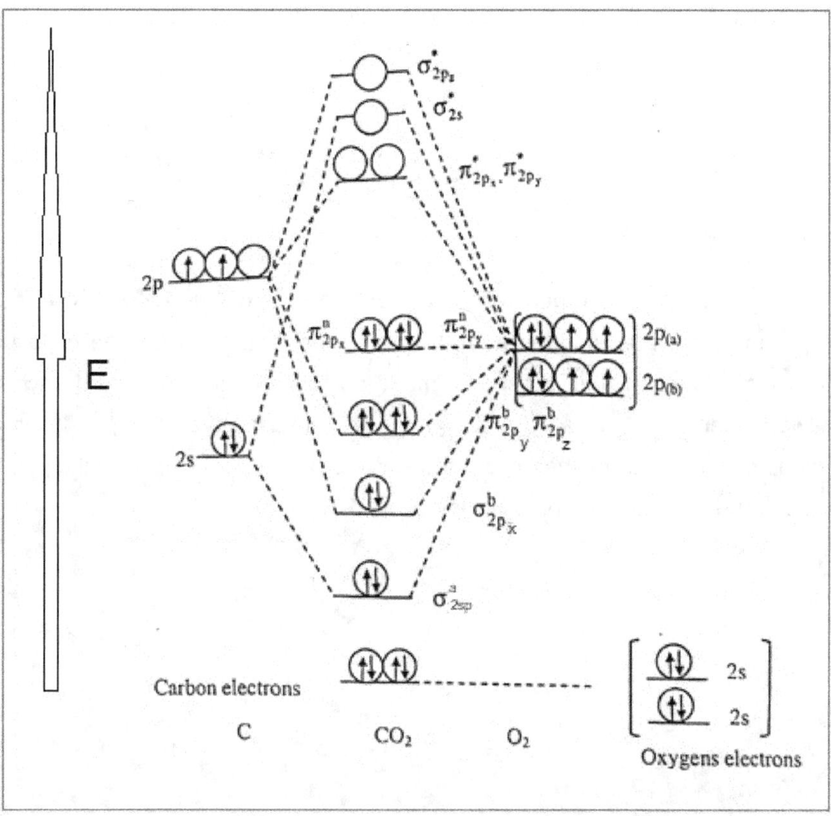

Figure 8.30: MO Energy level diagram of CO_2 molecule

The outer electron configuration of C is $2s^2$, $2p^2$ and that of O is $2s^2$, $2p^4$. The molecular orbitals for CO_2 molecule are obtained from valence orbitals. Thus,

MO energy level diagram for CO_2 molecule: The MO diagram for CO_2 molecule is shown in figure 8.30. The molecule contains 16 outer shell electrons, made up from six electrons from each of the two oxygen atoms and four electrons from the C atom. However, the 2s orbitals of oxygen and the electrons therein are too low in energy so they do not take part in bonding.

The CO_2 molecule contains two sigma and two pi bonds it their structure. It shows diamagnetic property since it does not contain any unpaired electrons.

8.15.2 Molecular orbital diagram for nitrogen dioxide (NO_2) molecule

It is an angular triatomic molecule. It is represented as

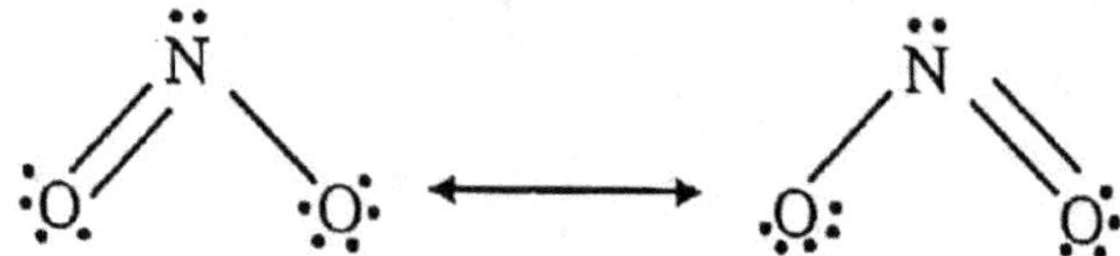

The outer electron configuration of N is $2s^2\ 2p^3$ and that of O is $2s^2\ 2p^4$. The MOs for NO_2 molecule are obtained from these valence orbitals. Thus, the molecule NO_2 contain 17 outer shell electrons, made up from six electrons from each of the two O atoms and five electrons from the N atom. However, the 2s orbitals of oxygen and the electrons therein are too low in energy so they do not take part in bonding. The MO diagram for NO_2 molecule is shown in figure 8.31.

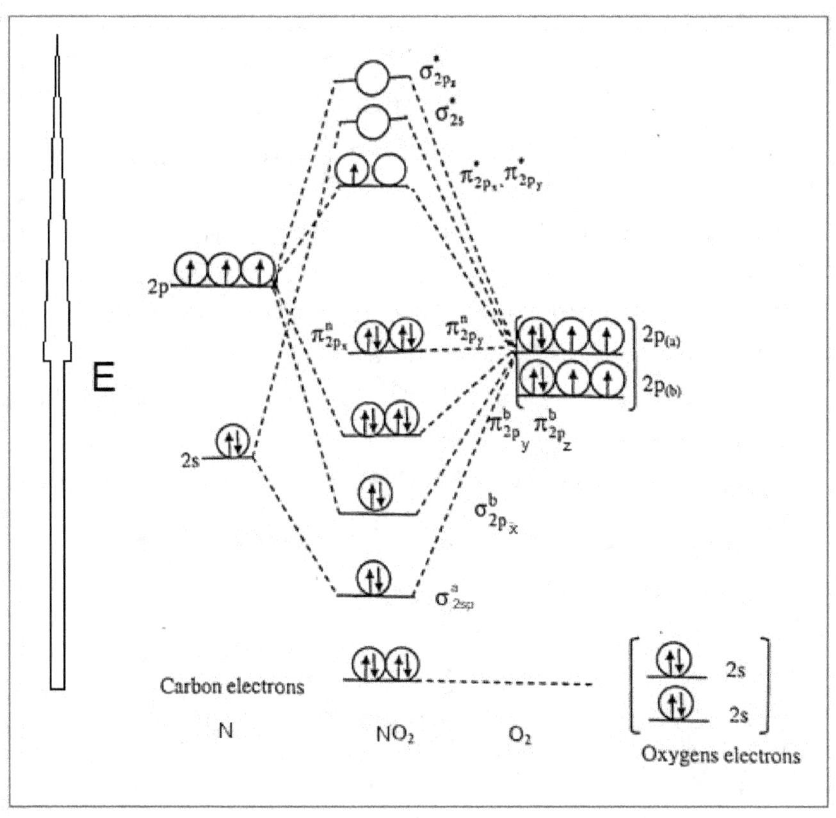

Figure 8.31: MO Energy level diagram of NO₂ molecul

REFERENCES

1) Concise Inorganic Chemistry by J.D. Lee - 5th edition
2) Co-ordination Compounds by Baselo and Pearson
3) Coordination Chemistry by A. K. De
4) Concept and Model of Inorganic Chemistry by Douglas – Mc Daniels - 3rd edition
5) New Guide to Modern Valence Theory by G.I. Brown - 3rd edition
6) Theoretical Inorganic Chemistry by Day and Selbin
7) Inorganic Chemistry - D.F. Shiver & P.W. Atkins, C.H. Longford ELBS - 2nd edition.
8) Basic Inorganic Chemistry - F.A. Cotton and G. Wilkinson, Wiley Eastern Ltd. 1992

ABOUT THE AUTHOR

Prof. Dr. Rajaram P. Dhok

M.Sc., M.Ed., M.Phil., Ph.D.

Savitribai Phule Pune University affiliated

Agricultural Development Trust's

Department of Chemistry, Shardabai Pawar Mahila

College, Shardanagar,

Malegaon Bk. Tal- Baramati, Dist- Pune, Maharashtra, India PIN – 413115

Prof. Dr. Rajaram Pandurang Dhok is currently working as Assistant Professor at Agricultural Development Trust's, Department of Chemistry, Shardabai Pawar Mahila College, Shardanagar, Malegaon Bk., Baramati, Pune, Maharashtra, India. He has almost 25 years of teaching experience. His research area is Quality of Groundwater and its use for Drinking and Agricultural Purpose. He has published several Research Papers in reputed International Journals. He is Reviewer of reputed International Research Journals. He has attended various International, National and State level Conferences, Workshops, Seminars and Presented Research Papers.

He has completed two Minor Research Projects funded by University Grants Commission (UGC), New Delhi. He has completed one Minor Research Projects funded by Savitribai Phule Pune University, Pune. He has written six books related to chemistry and Environmental Science. The names of book are Industrial Chemistry Published by Success Publication Pune, Climate Change: Causes, Consequences and Coping Strategies Published by International e–Publications, Collection of Articles in Chemistry Published by Applied Science Innovation Pvt. Ltd. India, Advances and Trends in Agricultural Science Published by Book Publisher International, Current Perspectives to Environmental and Climate Change Published by Book Publisher International, Groundwater Quality for Drinking Purpose online available on Amazon.com. He is Life Member of "Indian Association of Chemistry Teacher (IACT)". He is Research Guide in the subject Environmental Sciences for Savitribai Phule Pune University, Pune.